Redemption

Barbara Winkes

ISBN: 978-1-7781247-1-6

Cover art © May Dawney Designs

Created with Atticus

For D.

Chapter One

It's nothing short of a miracle that Kendall isn't behind bars, and that we're both still alive. I haven't given myself much time to process the recent events. I'm grateful we're here, able to pick up the pieces, or at least, some of them.

It's a bright summer day when I watch her lay the bouquet of long-stemmed roses on her parents' grave. She brought a smaller arrangement for her uncle as well. His is still overflowing.

I stay at a respectful distance. Kendall was able to leave the hospital this morning, and she asked to do this first. I am not in a hurry to get back to the mountain of paperwork, just as I'm sure she's not looking forward to never-ending meetings with lawyers and investigators.

But freedom doesn't come without a price.

Wearing jeans and a sweater, her hair in a ponytail, Kendall looks a lot more relaxed than when I first saw her, in church at her mother's funeral, pledging to fulfill Angela Mancini's dying wish to find out who killed her husband, Kendall's father. She was wearing a black dress back then, high heels, grief and vulnerability combined with a dangerous attitude. None of this is completely gone. She seems more serene, despite the recent challenges, and the ones that lie ahead.

Perhaps clarity makes all the difference. She'll have it soon, regarding her future, which will have an impact on my future either way. Clarity is a good thing.

I finally approach her. The doctors might have declared her well enough to go home, but she still needs to rest, not that I'll have much of an influence. A gunshot wound isn't something to mess with.

"Ready to go home?" I ask, and she straightens.

"Don't worry, Agent Johnson. I'm in no mood to run away."

"I'm glad to hear that. Let's go."

～ele～

There's not much I can do other than drop her off at home. I'll have to go back to work, and she has to meet with some people now. It's all related—after the capture of Jimmy Bruno, her father's former right-hand man, and the death of Tony Bianco, there's a lot to sort out, on her side, on mine. There's no point in obsessing over anything else.

Kendall is unusually quiet during the drive.

"Are you in pain?"

She shrugs. "The state hasn't taken all my money yet, so I can still afford some good drugs."

I must have hesitated for a moment because she chuckles. "All legally prescribed, don't worry. I have no intention of screwing this up."

"You saved my life. It's not going to be so bad."

"That's what you keep telling me, but I guess we'll have to wait and see."

This is just small talk, I know. She's not the type to wait and see. Kendall has her lawyers at the ready, and they are already at work ironing out the best deal possible for her.

Now Tony Bianco won't be able to testify, but I never trusted in him to tell a sliver of the truth. Jimmy Bruno—he will try to save his hide any way. It's not up to me to worry about Kendall. I have a job to do.

"I'll see you tomorrow, then," I say, when we arrive at the building that houses her condo.

"You will."

She smiles, leaning in, and for a moment, I worry she might kiss me in front of the two agents that followed us in the other vehicle. For an even shorter moment, I don't care. What is wrong with me? It's obvious I'm dealing with the near-death experience in a very different way. I'm not even the one who got shot.

"Have a good day, Robyn."

It still feels strange to have her say my name in this soft, intimate tone, stirring up memories of a time we both must forget about. Easier said than done.

"You too. Take it easy."

Somehow, everything I say seems to be amusing to her. I turn away, feeling righteously irritated. Against all odds and reason, still, intrigued.

If she has a long day ahead of her, mine will be even longer.

I have a few minutes to get another coffee before meeting with my boss and the prosecutor. My partner Hampton McKay is present as well as a couple of other agents. I notice that his tie is a bit crooked—he hasn't gotten a lot of sleep in the past weeks either.

I went undercover with the Mancinis, targeting head of the family Kendall Mancini with a two-fold strategy. One was to collect evidence for any crimes along the way, the other to find out more about the infamous raid that killed her father before she would declare a vendetta on a rival family, the Biancos. Both avenues were meant to convince her to cooperate, help bring down the more violent Biancos, and avoid an all-out war.

It got complicated, and not just because I got a lot closer to her than I imagined.

Regardless, we succeeded on those objectives, solved the murder of Alphonso Mancini and brought Kendall to the table. Tony's son Frank is in custody. There will be some more loose ends to tie up, but we made great strides in curtailing organized crime in the city.

If there's something the other people in the room still don't know, it's for the best. For all of us.

"So that will be it?" Hampton asks, incredulous. "She gets away with it all, doing no time?"

Ryan Farmer from Financial Crimes gives him a shrug. "My thoughts exactly, but you know her lawyers will go for that. I'm not happy with it either."

"We're not there yet," the AUSA informs us. "She destroyed government property, made an attempt to escape custody after a cooperation agreement."

She did that in order to save me. I don't, can't say it out loud, because even in my head it sounds ambiguous. Getting rid of Tony Bianco and the most relevant competitor mattered to Kendall, no doubt about it. What good did it really do for her when she was already in negotiations with the authorities? She could have stayed in her condo, leaving that ankle bracelet intact.

She didn't owe me anything...and vice versa.

"You're with us, Agent Johnson?" the SAC, Rachel Carr, asks, startling me out of my musings.

"Yes. Of course. I think it's reasonable...She will admit to everything we already have on paper, pay fines, and we get most of the Bianco clan. I think it's a win-win."

"I'm not sure I'd call it that, but it's something we can work with," the AUSA agrees, to my surprise. "Thanks to your work, Agent Johnson, we have a solid argument to make. Ms. Mancini knows that this time, there will be no second chances. I know you were hoping for more," he addresses Farmer, "but this is a good outcome. Those fines won't be pocket change."

Agent Farmer doesn't look too convinced, but she nods.

Everyone's mostly happy. There's no need for me to still feel restless and antsy, is there?

Chapter Two

I'm surprised the FBI lets me visit my parents' grave this morning. Perhaps that's their attempt to mellow me up a bit more, even when I've shown my soft side by saving one of their agents.

Was it my smartest decision? One could argue, but having Robyn alive and at the negotiating table serves everyone. That's all the motivation I can admit to because everything else is fantasy and innuendo. I never told the investigators that she crossed a line, for several reasons. It wouldn't be the worst idea to keep it as a last resort bargaining chip. Then again, I'm not even sure how much it would be worth. That, and I like the idea that there's something between us only we share, well, we and the rest of my family, but they have other things to think about right now.

Soon after I'm back home, I call in my lawyer, MacKenzie Winter and one of her associates, a woman named Ainsley Dunne. I have coffee and pastries delivered from a nearby coffee shop, because I think I've earned it, after bullets flying and having to deal with numbers that might hurt even more.

I have my housekeeper arrange everything in the living area by the window, move a couple of tables around. Comfort is key. For me, at this moment, anyway. Winter and Dunne are just lucky.

When the two arrive, we shake hands, then MacKenzie hugs me, a rare display of affection. When she first started to work for my family, the name Winter wasn't yet on the letterhead. We go way back, and I trust that she'll help me sort out the recent chaos.

"I'm so glad you're back home, Kendall," she says.

"Me too. We can finally get back to work. Sit, tell me how bad the damage is."

I'm not sure how to interpret her expression.

"Come on, it can't be that bad, right? I know Robyn got them some insights, but that was only the first layer."

"And we'll deal with that," MacKenzie says. "I'm confident that you won't have to do jail time."

"That's the least I expected. I gave them everything they asked for, and then some. How confident are you?"

"I don't think it's an issue. You saved the life of one of their agents. We can lean on that."

"Okay. What else?"

She exchanges a look with Dunne, and then says, "The judge that granted bail the last time? She won't be happy that you took off the moment you saw an opportunity."

"To save that agent, remember? I've got a hole in my shoulder to prove my goodwill."

"I know. You'll probably deal with an audit though, and some fines coming your way. On top of the back pay."

I straighten, and wince. "I expected that, too. It was part of the original deal. Robyn helped me find out who killed my father. I guess there is a price to that."

"Luca called me yesterday."

"Interesting that he calls you, and not me. I haven't seen him much at the hospital either. What did he say?"

"He wants to come by soon, discuss the future of the Mancini Group...and the rest of the business." I can tell she's uncomfortable, which makes me wonder if my cousin is going to be more of a problem than the FBI or the IRS.

"Claudia came by before I had to deal with Bianco. She made some similar noises. Am I looking at a hostile takeover?" I try to sell it as a joke, but it doesn't quite come across as such.

MacKenzie frowns, while Ainsley Dunne keeps her gaze fixed on her notebook. It's unnerving.

"They are worried, "MacKenzie says. "After losing your parents, and Lorenzo..."

Yes, Luca and Claudia have lost their father too, but that wasn't my fault. I fail to see what this has to do with the business.

"We are all still grieving. That doesn't mean there's any need for changes. I'm not going to prison. I'll still run the company."

"I tried to alleviate their worries, tell them that at this point, it's the best bet for the company and the family if you cooperate. No one will be poor."

"That's what I understood. But they aren't convinced? Look, I'm the one with the bargaining chips. They have the same liabilities and more. They should be happy I'm taking some heat off of them."

"That's what I've been trying to tell them."

"Try harder. I'm not retiring from any part of the business. Let them come in and fine me. I'll pay and get on with life."

MacKenzie nods, looking thoughtful.

"Can you do that? I need my family to have my back right now." It was bad enough to realize that Jimmy Bruno who had been around my family for two decades, was not who we thought he was.

For a few seconds, there's a laden silence between us, before MacKenzie says, "Luca has called some of our investors for dinner tonight. I think you should be there for it."

This might not mean what I think it does, but I'm still glad I'm sitting when she delivers the news.

"All right. Thanks for the update. I'll definitely be there. I guess I should clear it with the FBI."

"You should," she agrees.

Spending time in a hospital bed has not been in my favor, but they'd make a mistake counting me out yet. I'm ready to take back my place.

The doctors have advised me to rest, but who has time for that? The meeting with the prosecutors will be early tomorrow. Before that, I have to salvage what's left of my authority. In recent weeks, news about the company might have been vague and confusing for investors: My uncle was murdered. I got shot. There have been rumors about my cousins playing a bigger role now that Jimmy is out. I'll have to set everyone straight.

No pain, no gain...but I'm definitely in pain as I'm struggling to zip up my dress. Damn Luca. While I'm barely out of the hospital, he's taking investors to *Catania*, the family restaurant, to remind everyone of my great-grandparents' humble beginnings. It's smart. I think it will remind them of what could be lost, even more than if they met at the headquarters of the Mancini group, or one of our Adria restaurants. Our investors believe in tradition. Some of them have old-fashioned, not to say bigoted views.

I have never held back who I am. Not everyone can deal with that. I wonder if Luca is planning to make some changes in his personal life, now that his father who threatened to disown him, isn't here any longer. Not my business. I understand everyone wanting to do these things at a pace they're comfortable with.

REDEMPTION

What's going down at *Catania*, is my business, and I'm not going to let anyone take that away.

⸺ ℓℓ ⸺

The first part is easy. When I walk inside *Catania*, the first reaction is stunned silence, then my fabulous employees stop what they are doing to clap. This is not exactly what I expected, but it sets the tone nicely. I stop by some tables to greet regulars, some friends of my parents.

"Kendall, I'm so glad you're well," Maria Romano says, taking my hand. "We've been worried about you." I remember she and her husband sent a get-well card. I didn't get a card from Luca or Claudia, come to think of it. Some missed calls, encouraging words in voicemails.

We have everything under control.

We'll see about that.

In the area at the back of the restaurant, partly hidden from the normal business, Luca is offering a feast for the investors. It's like a scene from a Scorsese movie...including the surprise guests.

When I walk up to the table, my heels clicking on the tiled floor, conversations at the table come to a halt. The guests, mostly men, regard me with expressions ranging from friendly curious to openly hostile. Some of them, I saw the last time at my mother's funeral. I know who's who, and who are the ones that thought Dad would be better off forcing me to marry Jimmy Bruno, so a man could take the reins. For the life of me, I don't know why so many people have the idea men are better at stabilizing things. There's not a lot of proof out there in the world. Regardless, my father did no such thing, and since I'm the heir, they'll still have to deal with me.

Karma.

"Good evening, ladies and gentlemen," I say. "I'm happy to see you all. Please, enjoy your meal. We have a lot to talk about tonight."

Luca, who looked like he saw a ghost for a moment, jumps to his feet.

"Kendall! Come on, let me get you a chair. Should you even be up?"

"I'm fine," I say through gritted teeth though sitting down sounds good to me. "Let's take a moment while everyone is busy."

"Of course. We'll be right back," he tells the guests. "Like my cousin says, enjoy. Can I get you anything? Water?" he addresses me.

"I haven't had dinner yet, and you can get me some water with my Chianti."

Luca frowns. "Aren't you still on pain medication?"

"I'm not going to argue with you on this. It's still my restaurant...or did I miss anything important while I was in the hospital?"

His face reddens. Not a good sign.

"You should be home, recovering. Things are under control."

"You and Claudia keep telling me. If everything's fine, why meet with the investors?"

"Are you kidding me? You got shot, you're cooperating with the FBI—"

"To find my father's murderer and get the Biancos off our backs, remember?"

"Yeah, well, I know that, but people get nervous. We need to keep the business together, right? Especially now that Dad is gone too. We have to consolidate."

"I agree, but you haven't seen me trying to go after your share, and Lorenzo's."

He sighs. "That's not what's happening."

"Then explain it to me. I have time."

"I just wanted to reassure them that everything's stable, and that we are not looking at any more arrests. That's still the case, right?"

"No one's going to get arrested."

"You spent a night in a holding cell, remember?" He holds up a hand, anticipating the angry retort. "Come on, Kendall, you have to admit you made some serious mistakes. You got involved with an undercover agent, and you underestimated the danger Bruno presented."

I can't believe what I'm hearing.

"Is this you getting back at me for making you tell your father the truth? You decided you'd let Jimmy blackmail you. You helped him."

It's complicated.

"This is not about a grudge," Luca insists. "If anything, I'm glad my father and I could have that conversation before his death. Mama is all right with it. I'm trying to save what I can of my business, and by proxy, yours. A thank you would suffice."

He's not going to stop, I realize. I'll have to keep watching him.

"Let's have some food delivered to the agents as well. We'll be here a while."

I can't wait to have that glass of wine, maybe two. I'm not going to drive, and I'll need something to soften what's one blow too many.

Chapter Three

O nce at home, all I want is a hot bath and then sleep until it's time to get ready for tomorrow's meeting. It turns out I don't have that luxury. I completely forgot I was supposed to meet a small group of friends for a late dinner and drinks. I'd cancel, but it's late for that, and I promised.

I haven't seen them since before I started preparing for my undercover assignment...I guess I could go for an hour or so. At least the venue is casual, a bar a few blocks from my home. On my way, I pass by the place where I made first contact with Kendall.

Why do I keep thinking about her, like this? She has committed crimes, mostly of the financial kind, but it's not like those are victimless. Her family did display some honor, taking in an abused woman, running a foundation that does actual charity work and isn't a front for more illegitimate business. I did what I had to do, found a softer target, played Kendall's determination to find her father's killer—because of that, we are able to dismantle the Bianco clan.

Still. She's not innocent. I shouldn't feel guilty, but I do.

I first met the three women waiting for me at the bar counter in college, and we've taken care not to lose touch, even though all of us went into different careers.

"Look who's finally made it!" Emma slips off her barstool to hug me. "I'm so glad to see you, Robyn. We weren't sure you could make the time."

I feel even guiltier for almost coming up with a flimsy excuse.

"I'm glad to see you too. I can't stay long though."

"Our table is almost ready," Gillian says. "Enough time for another drink and for you to tell us what you've been up to."

Not that I can say much. And I didn't realize we had a table.

"A lot of work," I say with a shrug. "Where is that table?"

"A couple of blocks away at Adria. I know it's not our usual, but I felt like we should be treating ourselves. Who knows when we'll see each other next?"

I can't argue with that, and I am hungry. I'm also wondering what they'd say if they knew what I did. It's becoming a regular question, though one that I'd never ask. Gillian is a lawyer. Kitty and Emma run stores for stationary and greeting cards. I don't think they'd understand.

Tomorrow, I need to be alert and detached. Just as well that I have a little time-out before, right?

As the evening proceeds, I find myself drifting. Perhaps I need time, to reintegrate myself into a more regular life, Agent Johnson, working regular cases. I've worked undercover before, but it was never that difficult to cut ties. I blame Kendall who keeps hinting at those moments between the lines. As long as she does it, I'm not free, and she reminds me of the power she has. I can't have that. I'll have to find a moment to talk to her.

My friends are discussing the current sad state of the world. I'm tired, but even if I wasn't I feel like I don't have much to contribute, caught up in my dilemma. I excuse myself and find the restroom where I splash some water on my face.

God's honest truth? A part of it was beyond exciting. Not the part where I got beaten up, and abducted—twice—or the part where Kendall was shot and I held her, her blood spilling onto me. That was...horrible.

But there was a time when I could watch her at work, at home, a time when we got intimately acquainted, and I got a glimpse of the luxury life she was leading. My friends and I are comfortable, enough to spend an evening at an Adria restaurant and not feel the pain so much, but hers has always been a different world. An intriguing, sensual world of wealth...and lies.

Uncomfortable with where my thoughts are going, I check my phone and realize I missed several messages from Hampton. I call him back immediately.

"Hey," he says. "I have to say you'll be sorry you missed this. Mancini is laying down the law at *Catania's*. Quite impressive though unfortunately we can't accept a free meal."

"What are you talking about?"

"Cousin Luca called in the investors. Kendall decided everyone needed a reminder of who's in charge, for now. These are very interesting dynamics."

"She'll do whatever it takes to keep the business together."

"Indeed. We'll be able to use that tomorrow."

"That's great. Should I join you?"

"Party's kind of over. Sorry."

"No, that's okay. I'll see you tomorrow. Thanks for the heads-up."

"No problem. Good night."

I end the call, but don't return to the table right away. Kendall won't be happy about this. I don't have much sympathy for Luca Mancini for being on the receiving end of her wrath. I remember him well, standing in the corner, fidgeting nervously but making no move to stop Bruno.

Perhaps there's now a good chance we can stop them all.

I go back to my friends, but don't sit down.

"I'm really sorry, but something came up. I swear, I'll do better next time."

"You almost made it to dessert," Kitty remarks ruefully. "Don't be a stranger, okay?"

I'd be better off not making a lot of promises in the near future.

———

Kendall must be home right now. As I walk down the street, I fantasize about going to see her. What would I say to her in private? Stop...Stop what? I believe she's thinking about the business and her own financial future first and foremost. Some players might still be loyal to the Biancos. Her cousins have their own agenda as it seems.

Is it possible that what I thought I'm reading between the lines is all in my head? We had a deal. It's done. We give her something, she gives us something in return, and we can all move on with our lives.

I let myself down.

Did I let her down? Hampton is right, avoiding jail is a big deal. She should be grateful for that.

Is there anything else we need to say? I did visit her in the hospital. Tomorrow, we'll map out parts of the future. Will it finally be over?

I need to curb that fantasy. She's still recovering. I make a sharp turn and walk towards the front door of a bar only a block away from my home. I don't feel like silence yet.

At the counter, I order a glass of white wine, scoffing at the irony. I could indulge in a better one at Adria. Ironic how every place I go is associated with her. My father, a retired agent and childhood friend of Alphonso Mancini's, had warned me about the family and their charming ways. But he and Kendall's father were friends as children—he knows nothing. I can't share with anyone how much I wish things were different. At one point, Kendall suggested that we leave the country together, take all the money and run. Every once in a while, for a second or so, I wonder what that would be like.

Even if it's decided that she won't be serving jail time, it's not like I can ask her out once all of this is over.

It's not like she'd be interested.

Time to go home, even though it hasn't felt like one in weeks.

Chapter Four

R ecent experiences and revelations should make me feel anxious and trapped, but truth be told? It's the opposite. I feel free. It might have to do with the fact that Jimmy Bruno, a constant hovering shadow, is gone from my life. I have to give him credit for being good at pretending...Well, so was Robyn.

I can see the people in my life for who they are—my parents whom I still miss, who had this amazing love story. That remained untouched even knowing that my dad was willing to risk the family business by working with the FBI.

Jimmy who was obsessed with me until his obsession with power and money won.

Robyn, the undercover agent for whom I still harbor mixed feelings.

Luca and the rest of my family who doubt me—I assume that didn't start yesterday.

Knowledge is power. Clarity is freedom. When I walk into the field office, I do it with my head up high, the same way I walked into that investors' meeting. The latter, at least, put Luca in his place. They know better than to count me out now.

My confidence in here might have to do with the brilliant lawyers I have by my side, Winter and Dunne. Not only will I not go to prison, I don't expect my lifestyle to change...much. We will always keep *Catania* in the family. The Mancini Group provides the main income, but I intend to sell the Adria restaurants rather sooner than later.

This is on my mind when the agent leads me to a conference room where several people are seated already: The SAC whose name is Rachel Carr, the AUSA, a woman I haven't met yet, Hampton McKay, and Robyn Johnson. I allow myself a moment to appreciate her appearance, the power suit, just a hint of make-up, her hair in a bun. She looks a little pale, and I wonder if she gets much sleep these days.

The end of the Bianco clan, our tug of war with crimes and emotions, it's a lot.

I realize there's coffee and pastries which I find somewhat amusing.

"Good morning, everyone," Carr says. "Now that we're complete, let's begin."

The conversation will be recorded, I know. I chose an outfit slightly more casual than Robyn's, but still elegant—the look of someone who's trying to be non-intimidating but is still aware that this will exist for the ages.

The first part is between the attorneys, and it allows me to study Robyn a bit more. I can tell the exact moment when she becomes aware of my scrutiny, and tenses.

What does she think, that I'd blurt out intimate secrets in the middle of this meeting that could very well determine my future? I don't think so.

I know what you like. I made it happen too...a few times.

She studies the papers in front of her, avoiding my gaze as if aware of my thoughts. Joke's on me as it's getting really warm in the room.

"Before we pick up where we left off the other time, we'd like to emphasize that Ms. Mancini meant no harm, on the contrary." Dunne is a quiet, soft-spoken woman, but her words resonate. "She only had Agent Johnson's safety in mind."

Robyn frowns at her papers.

"Ms. Mancini," the prosecutor prompts, and I have to move on to less pleasant memories.

"Like Ms. Dunne says...Sofia came to see me after I was released. We talked. I had a suspicion, but I wasn't sure until Jimmy called me. Knowing what he'd done already, I knew there would be no second chances." I can see MacKenzie holding her breath, and add, "I wanted him alive, of course, to be held accountable. But more than anything, I knew that time was of the essence, and I had to act. He saw her as an obstacle to get to me, and Tony...Well, you know all about what a charming fellow he was, hiring Jimmy to get my father murdered."

That's the sanitized version, and it's all they need to know.

"It never occurred to you to go straight to the FBI?" McKay asks.

"I was afraid for Agent Johnson's life...and maybe I felt that since Bianco and Bruno got to her because of me, I should be the one to fix it. I'm not saying it was rational, but I didn't think of bail, or the consequences in general. I will gladly provide you with the funds to purchase a number of new ankle bracelets."

MacKenzie clears her throat. Okay. Too much. I swear I could see the hint of a smile on Robyn's face. The other woman, an agent with Financial Crimes, doesn't blink. I have a suspicion why. She probably thinks that too many people, who commit so-called white-collar crimes, get away with it. She's not wrong. I hold her gaze, mine a bit more daring than it should be given the situation.

She doesn't know me. I haven't always kept to the straight and narrow, but I also have few regrets. A good part of my money goes to important places. A part of it goes to my lifestyle. Sue me.

Well, that's what they're doing, but still.

"I am really sorry," I say. "I know that I should have handled this differently. Believe me, I had a lot of time to think, in the hospital—after getting shot. I think we're all on the same page here, wanting to get this over as quickly as possible. I gave you everything my father had on the Biancos. I hope that was useful for you. Contrary to what you might think, I didn't engage Jimmy to go around and intimidate people. We were trying to find Arturo Rossi when we spoke to Carlo. It turns out he is a murderer too."

We've talked about this. I don't want to ramble, but I also want to make sure I have the time to say what I need to say. I see the looks exchanged between the people on the other side, and all of a sudden, I feel nervous.

What if it's not enough?

What if they decide to throw the book at me and set an example?

Was this on my father's mind in the last hours of his life?

I pour myself a glass of water, forcing myself not to gulp it down.

"We're aware, thank you," the AUSA says. "We're certainly grateful that Agent Johnson is here at the table with us. I want to go back to the records she provided us with."

I lean back and let MacKenzie do her magic. Yes, Robyn was undercover, and she had all the paperwork at the ready, but some of it could still be interpreted as sketchy...The Financial Crimes agent, Farmer, has her lips set in a thin line.

"Ms. Mancini is ready to pay whatever fines the court sees fit, and pay back any taxes that might have been missed..." I can't help but wince. I wouldn't mind paying my "fair share" if we weren't still too much governed by anti-choice and anti-LGBT BS, and the people who find it easy to agree to disagree on these subjects. As long as that's the case, and too much of my tax money is going to ignorance, I bristle at this. But, of course, it's better than prison. It's hard to argue with that.

"It's true," I acknowledge. "I want to do better, and I promise I'll see to it that my accountants are better equipped in the future. I understand you'll need some guarantees regarding my compliance. I'm willing to give them to you. I hope you're not seeking to shut down the Mancini Group. Along with the office buildings, we provide residential homes and affordable housing as well. These aren't just words. Our buildings are beyond reproach."

MacKenzie kicks me lightly under the table. Robyn looks intrigued, and I'm irrationally glad she doesn't seem to be mad at me any longer.

"So, you would be willing to have one of our agents oversee your compliance regarding business practices?" Carr asks mildly. "You'd give Agent Johnson access to everything she needs?"

Oh, this is going to be unexpectedly fun, and more complicated.

"Of course. That might be helpful in many ways...If she wanted to go into Interior Design for real." Her cheeks redden. "I'm sorry about that. Yes, I want to show you that I'm turning over a new leaf. It makes sense that Agent Johnson will be there for it, right?"

"Okay," Carr says, amused.

Great. It seems like a good idea to have her on my side, to some extent.

"There's one more thing."

I'm not surprised. There always is.

After the meeting, I pay a quick visit to headquarters, mostly to show my face and assure everyone that I'm not dead and won't be going to prison either. Business, mostly, as usual—except the FBI will be around for a little while longer. Nothing to worry about.

I work from home for the rest of the day, grudgingly take a much-needed nap and then meet Luca at *Catania* for dinner.

"Nothing can keep you down for long," he says, a strange greeting, I think.

"Don't sound so disappointed."

"Come on, Kendall. We're all happy you're back."

There are many things I could say to that, but I want tonight to stay within polite boundaries. I might not like it, but after Uncle Lorenzo's death, Luca is the one who owns the most shares after me. I can still do whatever I want, but it might be strategically smarter to involve him in some of those conversations and decisions.

"That's good to know. Look, you know I'm still somewhat out of commission. I wanted to have a relaxed dinner...but I also wanted to update you on some of the recent developments. The FBI is very happy arresting members of the Bianco clan, so they will go somewhat easy on us. They wanted something in return, of course. I've been careful. We'll still have to pay."

"I expected that, but to be honest, you probably made it worse by not staying in your condo as the judge ordered."

Of course.

"You and I both know that Jimmy is an opportunist. He would have gotten her killed."

Luca shakes his head.

"Let me get this straight, Bianco had her, and Bruno went after her...and you had to get in the middle of it? You could have put yourself in a much better position. She's not your friend. She set you up."

"She also helped me find out who murdered my father. Yes, she set me up, but I wasn't going to let a couple of sexist assholes kill her."

He winces at that. I'm not sure it's my choice of words, or if he's remembering the time he teamed up with Bruno, the other time Robyn was in mortal danger.

"That part is done, and I'm glad it is. Agent Johnson will come to headquarters tomorrow, and on a few other days, and she'll have access to everything she needs. That's part of the deal."

"Kendall. You're basically handing it all over."

"You know I'm not. This is part of why I wanted to talk to you. Uncle Lorenzo kept things clean within his shares of the Mancini Group, right? So, you have nothing to worry about."

I wait, wondering if I'm going to learn anything new and disturbing. When he doesn't answer, I say,

"There's something else. We don't have the exact numbers yet, of course, but I'm thinking about selling Adria."

"You want to do what? You've got to be kidding me!"

Now we're getting somewhere. I think.

"Actually, no, I'm serious about it. We'll always keep *Catania*, for sure, but the concept for Adria is completely different. If we wanted to grow in this area, we'd have to invest a lot more time and money, and now's not a good moment. Slimming down, focusing on the real estate makes a lot more sense. And we could re-invest some of that money."

27

"No. Kendall, no, you can't do this. This is exactly what we were talking about when we said you should take a step back. After what happened to your parents, and now with that agent, you're too close to all of this. Let us help."

"I don't need help. I need to make smart business decisions and getting rid of Adria is one of them. Unless you know something I don't."

"What's that even supposed to mean? You know everything that's going on in the business, right? We have some influential people tied up in Adria."

"The new owners would inherit those influential people, so what's the problem?"

"Do I really have to spell it out for you?"

"Apparently, because I have no idea what you're talking about."

"Don't be silly. You know that not all the money comes from people who are there to eat ridiculously expensive food."

I'm not sure how to react. This is a lot more troubling than it could be helpful in the long run. I didn't think Lorenzo and his family would be so blatant. Is that what Claudia was trying to tell me?

"Well, I've always preferred comfort food anyway. Let's do the math in the next few days and get a feel for what we could do."

"You can't move this fast."

"I'm not going to do anything rash. I just want to get the ball rolling."

He doesn't answer.

I take another bite of my pizza and fill my glass once more thinking about that foolish moment when I thought Robyn and I had the semblance of a future. She, too, liked the comfort of *Catania*.

Chapter Five

The universe wants to torment me, I'm sure. Why give me that assignment? After the recent months, I would have been more than happy with something less high-profile.

Ryan Farmer isn't all that happy either. She was probably sure she'd get it, watch Kendall and bust her if there was so much as a hint of wrongdoing.

I have to admit it makes sense—I know Kendall and her business better than anyone. Being near her a lot more in the future is going to be tricky, and not because I plan to look the other way, on the contrary. I hope there won't be anything to report, that she's learned her lesson. But do people who grow up with all this entitlement ever learn?

I guess I'm going to find out. I can't stall any longer.

Tomorrow, we're going to fall back into our respective roles. Before that, I need answers. That part can't wait.

I leave the office when I feel prepared enough for the next day.

At home, I shower and change, and have a quick bite before I call a cab. Whatever it is that's left between us, Kendall enjoys this play of seduction, including food and wine, and I don't want to give her too much room.

Or do I?

When I ring the doorbell, I'm buzzed up right away. I wonder if she'll be able to keep this condo after all the numbers are crunched.

Kendall doesn't look concerned at all.

"Agent Johnson, please come on in. Could I interest you in a nightcap?"

"No, thank you." Once again, I can't help being impressed by the view. Perhaps I need something to distract myself when she helps me out of my coat, and a whiff of her perfume brings up complicated memories. "There I thought we were already on a first name basis."

"We were...Jess."

Oh yes, I deserved that.

"You're right. Given the job I'll be doing in the near future, it's better not to appear too friendly."

"Appearances matter," she agrees with a smile. "Except it's just the two of us now, and I checked the condo for bugs. There are none. So, what brings you here?"

If only I knew, if only I could be honest with myself, and by proxy, her.

"I wanted to see how you're doing."

"You know. Recovering, doing my best to keep the business together while my family tries even harder than the FBI to destroy it."

"I'm sorry," I say, a quick, automatic response.

"Are you?"

"For the family part anyway. The rest of it is just about the law."

She studies me curiously, long enough for me to turn away. "You didn't come here this late to update me about the law, did you? Because we're long past that."

"You want the truth," I say as I stare at the lights of the city, "I don't know. I keep trying to understand why you haven't told anyone. You enjoy holding that over me?"

To my surprise that makes her laugh.

"I said something funny?"

"Yeah, you did," she says behind me. "The thought might have occurred to me, but at this point, I don't think I'd get more than a yawn out of your boss or the AUSA. I have my lawyers to try and make me look as good as possible in this mess. Saving an agent's life makes me look a whole lot better than being so desperate and lonely I fell in bed with said agent the first opportunity I got."

I'm laughing too.

"You have such a way with words."

"Not my only talent...As you know."

I turn around, realizing with a start that she is standing very close.

"You saved my life. I'm grateful for that," I say. "I wonder if you did it so you could mess with my mind."

"I admit it's fun, but no. I couldn't let them get away with it, especially Tony."

"Yeah, Tony. You swore you'd bring down your father's killer, and you did. Was he always going to end up dead, even if he hadn't abducted me and planned to kill me?"

She gives this more thought than I had expected.

"Does it matter now? He did all those things and more, and frankly, I'm not sad he's gone, or that Frank is behind bars with the rest of them. If I need to pay those fines so all of it could happen—all right with me."

Kendall takes another step. I take one back.

"I came for you," she says. "So I could mess with your mind. And so I could do this." She leans in to kiss me, a soft touch of lips on lips at first that soon gets a lot more intimate and passionate. By the time I pull back, we're both breathless, and she's wearing a smug smile.

"I can't do this."

"Not right now, in any case," she agrees. "Give me a little bit more time, and we can...reconvene."

"That's not what I meant, and you know it," I fire back, irrationally angry. It's not like she forced me to come here—or kiss her back like my life depended on it.

"Don't worry. I understood exactly what you meant."

I shake my head in frustration and flee.

Whatever happens tomorrow, I just made sure it will be more difficult than necessary.

Or perhaps she's right and I knew what I was doing.

I'm not sure which would be worse.

The next morning, Kendall acts like nothing ever happened, and I'm not sure if it's a blessing or a curse. If seems like nothing much can touch her when she's in her element, at headquarters of the Mancini Group, or in her luxury condo. In fact, I almost feel like I'm an employee here as she shows me around once more.

Around eleven a.m., she decides we should take a break in her office. Luca Mancini drops by and soon leaves after we share an icy greeting.

Funny, you'd think I'm the one who beat *him* up.

Kendall's gaze is pensive. "You could have pressed charges," she says.

"I could have. But you might have seen that we are a little busy, not that it takes away from what he did. Jimmy is stonewalling, whatever good that'll do for him, but if he decides to talk, that might make a difference."

"Yeah."

"That's all you have to say on the subject?" I ask, intrigued. "I can't seem to figure it out. You let Jimmy run..."

"...because you were hurt, and I thought it was more important to take care of you at the time. I was sure the FBI would get to him at some point."

"You didn't turn Luca in."

"Again, I had other things on my mind. I certainly won't stand in the way if you want to hold him accountable. In his defense...I'm not sure I like saying that...I don't think he knew where Jimmy was or that he was in bed with the Biancos. Luca was afraid that Uncle Lorenzo might find out about his arrangement with Elena." She shrugs. "In the end, Lorenzo didn't mind so much as long as appearances were kept up. Go figure, he and Dad grew up in the same family, but their takeaway was quite different."

It is all fascinating, but of course I'm not here for a deeper look at the Mancini family history.

"How are you doing with this?" I ask, making a sweeping gesture. "I mean...You're not the kind of person who's used to limits."

Kendall pours another cup of coffee for each of us.

"Somehow, I don't think this is the kind of question you'd ask any of your targets...witnesses...whatever it is I am to you at this point."

"I wouldn't. But I'd like to know, and it makes my job easier if you don't plan to play hide and seek with your records."

"We have an audit coming," she says. "I will hunker down with Accounting and make sure everything is in order. That night in the holding cell was quite enough. Orange would not be my color."

"What makes you different? I mean, you'll be getting away pretty unscathed."

Kendall starts laughing. "Have you considered the possibilities? People have been floating numbers around me, and the state is coming for a big chunk of my money."

"Pocket money."

"Not really, but I think that's beside the point. You of all people know how it works. Your partner doesn't like it, and the lady from Financial Crimes doesn't, but they'll cut me some slack because I delivered them a few people who are worse. Frank Bianco refused to divorce Sofia after she fled from his abuse. He had a couple of mistresses, and I doubt he treated them any better. Jimmy, Tony...You had a couple of run-ins with them. I only regret that it took me so long to see Jimmy for the psychopathic asshole he is."

"So, you're really a good person, misunderstood, maybe."

"I try not to be a horrible person. That might be a low bar, but I still think it's more than a lot of people can say for themselves. Why are you so angry at me? Do I have to remind you I was the one who got shot?"

She's yanking my chain, I know.

"No, you don't. I remember it well."

"You didn't answer my question. What's with the anger? I can't be the worst you've ever come across."

I think I'm mostly angry because she has a point, sees through my defenses.

"Maybe I'm angry at myself. I don't need to tell you that this got far out of hand."

Kendall's gaze is calm, interested, a stark contrast to my inner turmoil.

"Don't be so hard on yourself. You had to be believable...and you were."

Do I detect sarcasm? Regret? Or are those simply reflections of my own emotions?

"Thanks...I guess."

"I have a meeting in ten minutes," she says, now back to being all business. "I assume you want to attend to make sure I don't do any shady back door deals?"

"Sure." I hesitate.

Kendall smiles. "How about tonight, you take a good look at the books of *Catania*? The agents refused wine the other day, and I almost didn't get them to eat, but in the end they were glad they did. You have to eat sometime too."

"I'd love that." Who knows what will happen to *Catania* once this is all over? I'll be selfish. The food is just too good. Just like the agents, I intend to pay for my meal. Keep the receipts.

"Good. And before we go in, I think you should know that Luca and I have decided to sell the Adria restaurants. It's better that way for everyone—and less paperwork for the FBI and IRS to go through."

I follow her out of the room, shaking my head. Why do I have the feeling that she's always one step ahead?

Chapter Six

There's no point in putting off necessary decisions, especially when my heart was never in Adria. It was a project of my grandparents, though like my great-grandparents, they still worked and cooked at *Catania*, and were passionate about the business. My parents made sure to keep it growing, but their focus was always on the Mancini Group first.

I always thought that *Catania* was a place where I'd see my own grandchildren run around at some point in the far future. The other restaurants never had that feel for me, and so I have gathered my, to a certain point, trusted, chief officers this morning.

"First of all, thank you all for being here. I'd just like to give you a heads-up on a couple of subjects. You may have noticed Ms. Johnson. I'd like all of you to give the investigators what they need. We are fully cooperating. Unfortunately, it's come to my attention that Mr. Bruno stole from the company and worked with our competitors, so it's most important that we get to the bottom of it."

Robyn's jaw drops a bit. I'm not sure if it's because I neglected to mention her job title, or because I still know how to run my business. Yes, they know that an FBI investigation is still underway, the audit is coming, and they're supposed to cooperate. If I lay a bit more of the blame on Jimmy, it's because I think he's earned it.

He took my parents from me.

He almost took my livelihood...and Robyn. Yes, I feel entitled to twist the truth the tiniest bit, make him look worse to make myself look better.

"I don't expect much to change in day-to-day operations." That elicits a wry smile from her. She was right earlier. I don't do limits very well. I know that in order to keep myself out of prison, I'll have to be careful. But I bank on the fact that previously, I've been surrounded by misogynist men who have committed far worse crimes.

"Something else I wanted to talk about is the Adria Group. Sandra, I'd like you to get together with accounting and get me the numbers for the past year. We are going to sell those restaurants."

"I'll get right on it," Sandra, the CFO, answers. "I assume...Luca is one of the people to talk to? Since Adria was mostly Lorenzo's responsibility."

"Yes, I'm aware. Luca and I have agreed that selling is the best way to consolidate, increase capital and reassure stockholders."

"You really think it sends the right message? It could look like the opposite if we're selling now." Sandra's criticism is a bit more subtle than Luca's has been. It comes as no surprise that it's a man who openly questions my decision.

"Not if we control the messaging. It's decided."

I want to get this done as soon as possible, not just because I think it's a good decision—which it is. I am more worried about the things Luca neglected to tell me regarding Adria. I'd prefer to get rid of those locations before anyone could get ideas. Anyone like...Robyn.

I want to run the business that my parents intended. If that means to come clean about certain things, so be it.

I'm paying my dues. At some point, the bleeding has to stop, doesn't it?

I'm not sure yet when that moment will come.

ele

Once everyone has left the room except for Robyn and I, I sink into a chair and pour myself some water. Appearances matter, but a whole meeting in these heels makes me want to cry. Every one of my male employees wears comfortable shoes. At least we pay everyone the same for the same job here, but still.

"Are you okay?" Robyn asks softly.

I make a dismissive gesture and take another sip.

"You know, when the hospital let you go home, what they meant was that you should continue to rest."

"Sure." I make a face at her. "You've met everyone. Do you really think I can afford to let things go any longer? The time in the hospital was bad enough. They stepped up best they could, but now I have to deal with Luca as well."

"We don't have to have dinner. Go home as soon as you can, take the evening."

"It hurts a lot more than I thought it would."

"The gunshot wound?"

"No, finding out everyone is out to get me. Of course the gunshot wound. Did you ever get shot?" I hope my tone is light enough for her not to take offense. The truth is she has nothing to do with my gloomy thoughts concerning Adria.

"Once, a flesh wound. That was bad enough. I sympathize."

"Thank you. And no, it's a good thing to go out for dinner. I'm home alone, I sleep too much, and I have nothing to distract me when I'm awake."

"Glad to be distracting."

"You are, no doubt about it."

It's her who changes the subject this time. "Would you ever think about selling *Catania* as well?"

"Oh no, never if I can help it. You'd have to pry those keys from my cold dead hands...You know it's been in the family for four generations, and I'd like to make sure there'll be a few more."

"You want children?"

"That's an awfully personal question for someone who's supposed to oversee my finances," I chide. Her smile tells me she knows I'm not all that serious. "There hasn't been much time to think about it in the past few years, but yes, I'd still like to have a shot at being a parent. I can't imagine I'd be so bad. I grew up with a pretty good example. What about you, Agent Johnson?"

"Now you're calling me Agent? Anyway, yes, I've been thinking about it. It would not be easy, and fairly expensive, but I could imagine it...With the right person."

"That goes without saying, doesn't it?"

"It does. I couldn't imagine doing it all alone." She gets up and comes to sit in the chair next to me. "I really look forward to dinner, but first of all I need you to tell me something."

"If I want to have kids with you?"

"Kendall, I need to know why you think you have to sell Adria yesterday. We can't have any surprises."

Damn. Every once in a while, I forget about the job she is here to do. Still. In my mind, I weigh how much I can tell her.

"You're right. Let's get this over with."

40

REDEMPTION

I steal away to the private bathroom attached to my office, let the water run and take in my reflection, not too happy with what I see.

I'm still in pain, and it shows. This was not how I wanted to proceed with the evening. Fortunately, it's time for medication though I might have to go easy on the Chianti. As if that wasn't enough, I just withheld a significant part of the truth from Robyn, a part that should never come out. I don't care much about Luca at this point—he tied himself to this kind of business practices, and that had nothing to do with him coming out or not.

There could be danger down the line, and before that happens, I need to get rid of those restaurants, be good Kendall, the one that gives up the bad guys and stays clear of them. So she can live happily ever after. I make a face at my mirror image. I've only been back at work for the second day, and I'm already juggling too many balls.

Will it ever end?

Is it up to me? I know that Luca and Claudia are watching me, to be supportive when needed maybe, or for signs of weakness that would mean they could take over. I'm not sure though about Claudia's and Elena's involvement in Adria. If they have any stakes in the group, my vision of an all-woman badass business association is quickly going down the drain.

Meanwhile, Robyn is waiting for answers, and dinner. I think I was able to stall her on the answers. Now I have to make sure she thinks I'm up to spending an evening in my favorite place. It still is, regardless of how many nights I've sat with Jimmy discussing business. That part, he was actually good at. Of course, now I know that all of it was for his own self-interest, and I just happened to benefit.

"Dad, how did you figure this would go?" I mumble.

"Kendall? You're okay in there?"

"I'm fine, just a minute," I call back in response to Robyn's concerned question. I turn off the faucet and quickly brush up my make-up. I have a plan. I'm not going to let a little pain ruin my day. That's just not me.

I look back into the mirror. Better. Things are under control. A few weeks from now, maybe I can talk her into a vacation, but first I'll see what I can talk her into tonight.

In the parking lot, Robyn walks straight to her car. She turns to me when I don't follow right away.

"I'll be back tomorrow, remember? I can drive you home and pick you up in the morning."

"That seems a bit outside of your job description..." I sense that I'm losing her and make myself move. "It's a good idea. Anyway, I'm too tired and hungry to think of a better solution."

"It's been a long day," she says, jiggling the keys in her hand. "I look forward to whatever's on the menu."

The way to a woman's heart is via good old-fashioned Italian food, even if said woman is still looking for a reason to put me behind bars. I'm fairly confident that it won't happen.

I have a plan. For everything.

Sofia is at the *Catania* tonight with a friend. We stop to say hello and then retreat to the usual table. Robyn's gaze is pensive. Maybe she's thinking of the first time I brought her here. Maybe she is, like I am, wondering what the rest of the night could bring. I am exhausted. I refuse to acknowledge that reality. A little blissful ignorance goes a long way in this context.

When the waitress arrives, I simply order a selection of appetizers, pizza, and a bottle of wine. Robyn's quizzical gaze gives me pause.

"What?"

"Nothing," she says, then reconsiders. "I just never know whether I should be annoyed or intrigued when you take charge like that. I know you know the restaurant better than anyone else, and everything will be delicious. I might want to study the menu a little bit more in the future."

"But my plan is working. You just said you want to come back in the future."

"I don't think I have much of a choice whether to stick around...and I cannot argue with this place."

"I'm so glad I have something that you want."

She doesn't deny it.

"For the record, the story about the small family business, you sell it well. Almost makes a person forget about the size of the business you really run."

"Yeah, maybe. It's for real though. My grandparents built Adria and turned Mancini Construction into the Mancini Group with the help of my parents. *Catania* is the constant for everyone."

"Children and grandchildren."

"That's the plan."

Andrea, the waitress arrives with the wine and appetizers, and I raise my glass. "To the future. With fewer to no bullets flying."

Robyn gives me a soft smile. "I have no trouble drinking to that."

Being at *Catania* is an immense comfort as usual, but I can't deny the signs. Tonight is likely not going to turn out the way I'd hoped. Some things you can't rush, but I'm not sure how much time I have before this ends. Worst case scenario, I wasn't careful enough, and Robyn, or the tax investigators will still stumble across something they shouldn't. Best case scenario, she'll finish her work and then...leave. I'd be fooling myself thinking that will have no impact on me. I might go back to inconsequential hook-ups—there's no one left to judge me. I might even earn some admiration for my battle scar. I don't want her to go, and the fact that I really do like to mess with her is only part of the reason.

We try a bit of everything before the pizza arrives, and we make room for the huge plate.

"This is so good." Robyn makes a sound I find slightly inappropriate when it comes to food, and it makes me even more aware of plans unlikely coming to pass tonight. Damn Tony Bianco messing with me from the grave. At least, I'm here. He's not.

"Do you think I could come back here after the case is closed, or will I be *persona non grata*?"

"Why would you think that? Of course, you can always come here."

I'd be a bit disappointed if she brought a new girlfriend, but we're not there yet. It might be the mix of pain medication and wine. I feel a bit more optimistic. Perhaps there is a time and place to reveal the whole truth, and a possibility that we could be on the same side. I might just be getting drunk.

"Good to know. This has become my favorite place in the city. I might bring you enough business to make up for the back taxes you'll have to pay."

"The last word hasn't been spoken yet, but I'm glad to hear that. I know you had sex with me for only one reason, and that kind of sucks, but you being here has changed a lot. I took a good hard look at whom I could trust. Not many people are left."

"Sofia is one of them," Robyn observes, not denying the charge. Like me, she has a complicated relationship with truth and attraction.

"Yes, absolutely. She never forgot what my parents did for her. She supported me in cooperating with the FBI even if there's a chance they could look at her work too. My family...You know how that turned out."

"You shouldn't let them push you out. For better or worse...you do most of the work."

"I guess you're right about that. But I'd like to change the subject if you don't mind. Work isn't going anywhere." I hold up the bottle that's still about one third full. "How about we finish this at home?"

She can't really admit it out loud any longer, but I know she enjoys being at my condo. We'll see where we can go from there.

Chapter Seven

So far it's been going...okay, I guess. I probably can't blame Kendall for the constant innuendo given the way we started out. Given the fact that I can't stay away. I mean, she's my responsibility, right? Our main witness to deliver more blows against organized crime, I have to make sure she's okay.

I don't have to feel guilty about dinner, or a glass of wine in the luxurious surroundings of her condo.

Perhaps I should feel guilty when she puts the glass aside and pulls me close for a kiss. I'm not even that surprised this time. I do have a moment of reason.

"We shouldn't be doing this...While you're still recovering." The second part elicits a knowing smile. Damn it, she sees right through me.

"Can you blame me for being impatient? I had a near-death experience. I really want to feel something better."

"You should rest. We're going to start early again tomorrow."

"I can rest once I have my life back together. Not that it's going to be anything like before." She sits back down and shakes her head. "It's hard to remember what I thought might happen once all of this came out, but it sure isn't anything like that. Closure...It's a big deal."

"That's why you should take care of yourself first," I say. I can be reasonable.

"You might have a point," she concedes. "I should get ready for bed and stay in there for a few hours, for a change." Kendall gives me a long look. "Obviously what I hoped was going to happen isn't on the menu tonight...Would you still stay a little bit longer?"

"Tuck you in?" I ask, feeling oddly touched.

"I'd love that."

"Sure, you go ahead. I'll just enjoy the view in the meantime."

"If you'd like anything else, you know where the fridge is."

"Thanks, but I'm fine."

She nods and heads for the bedroom while I turn my gaze to the window, wishing...It's hard to say where I would want to be, if not here, and that is alarming. At least there are still ways I can justify my behavior, my feelings for her. She's trying to do the right thing, even if I, not to mention the law, disagree on how to get there.

But that bullet was meant for me.

That might the thing hardest to get over.

Kendall comes out of the bathroom, her hair slightly damp, rolled up in a bun. She's wearing a robe. My breath catches in my throat when I realize she's not wearing anything underneath it.

"You promised," she reminds me.

"Yes. I remember."

I follow her into the bedroom where she chooses panties and a tank top from different drawers and...

"What? You've seen me naked before."

"I have." My gasp might have been more from the sight of the dressing over the wound, though I can't say for sure. It looks clean and not that threatening, but it's a reminder. "It's just that...I wish this wouldn't have happened."

That sounds ominous. Fortunately, she understands.

"But it did, and I guess we both have to get over it. We know we've been operating in a high-risk environment. Things like that happen."

They do. Humans are fragile. I hate to acknowledge that.

She pulls back the covers and slips under it. I step closer and cover her, hesitating.

"Would you stay for a bit?"

"I can't," is my first, instinctive response.

"Who do you think I'm going to tell?" That's a good question indeed. Aside from the flying bullets, going back to the day-to-day reality of the job hasn't been that bad. I still have a job.

I lie down next to her on top of the covers. Seducing, soft covers. I can't suppress the yawn. "I can't sleep here."

"I'm not asking you to. Just stay for a few minutes?"

I guess I can do that, given what she has done for me.

I'm not sure what the original plan was. This wasn't it, for neither of us...but it feels so good.

I might feel much too safe in these surroundings, because when I wake, it's because Kendall is gently touching me. Not in a sensual way, though I could imagine the mood shifting within a heartbeat.

"I hate to wake you," she says, "but if we get up now, we can have breakfast before we have to leave, and still have time to drop by your apartment."

"Yes. Of course." I'm too well rested to be embarrassed. Really, what's the damage to anyone? Kendall is complying with the investigation. This will be over soon. I might have conflicting feelings, about her, about what she'll get away with, and the worry that she might not—but things are going the way they should. Nothing to worry about.

ℓℓℓ

We spend the following days pretty much the same we did the first. To my relief and disappointment, Kendall immerses herself in work and preparing the sale of Adria. She doesn't invite me to *Catania*, or over to her condo.

I hear Luca yell a lot, but the chief officers have all rallied behind her, so there's not a lot he can do.

This relative distance is giving me a lot of time to think about my future once this case is over. It's not a bad thing.

That makes it even more of a surprise when one evening, Kendall turns to me and says, "I'd like to meet with your parents sometime soon. Your father in particular."

I have my coat and keys in hand, nearly drop the latter. "What? Why?"

We are alone in her office after another grueling meeting in which Luca made a last-ditch effort to avoid the sale of the Adria Group. There are now two interested buyers.

Kendall regards me patiently, but I have no clue.

"Your dad came to visit me before my bail hearing."

"You never told me about that."

"I didn't mean to keep it from you. A lot of things happened shortly after that. I'd just like to talk. It seems like he knew my father at a young age. And he was in touch shortly before his death."

"Okay. I understand," I say even though that's debatable. I know one thing for sure. Kendall doesn't make requests like this without purpose. "I can ask him. He's retired as you know, so there shouldn't be a problem."

"You can check in with your colleagues, but I don't think it's any more improper than the things we've already done."

"Yeah, I know what you're doing. It's been a while since we've done anything improper, so it's not working as much."

"You're no fun," she comments. "All right, how soon can you ask?"

"I could call now," I offer, and I swear I startled her. "Too soon?"

"Maybe. I don't know. I promise you there's no hidden motive. It's just that so many people have told me stories about my dad...I think this would clear up some things."

"Okay. Let's do it then. I don't know what they have planned for the week, but I'll find out." I make the call while Kendall waits, looking nervous.

Dad picks up.

"Hi Robyn! How are you?"

"I'm good. Listen, I have Kendall...Kendall Mancini here with me."

"You didn't need a last name," he says, amused.

"I guess not. Kendall would like to talk to you some more about her dad. You think you could make the time?"

The silence lasts a bit longer than I would have liked.

"It's private, unrelated to my work. It would mean a lot to her."

"I guess we can arrange something." His tone is cautious.

"How about we come over to dinner...tomorrow, or the day after, whatever works better for you."

"Tomorrow is good," he says and chuckles. "I think I was just surprised at the idea of you bringing Kendall Mancini to dinner. I assume you know what you're doing."

"I do," I say, feeling my cheeks heat. "We'll bring some wine."

"Sounds good. Tomorrow at six?"

"We'll be there. Thank you." I end the call and look at Kendall who has followed the conversation with tense interest. "Tomorrow at six. You think we could get some of that Chianti from *Catania*?"

"I'll make sure of that. Thank you so much, Robyn."

She steps forward and embraces me, and I don't search for a hidden meaning. This is going to be off the clock, for both of us—a family dinner.

Dad was right, there is something remarkable about it.

Rachel Carr finds it interesting as well when I share Kendall's request with her.

"It will be just an informal dinner. She has some questions about her father that mine might be able to answer."

Giving this some thought, Rachel answers, "I can't see anything wrong with that as long as it stays on topic. Your father knows better than anyone what's at stake."

"I'll make sure it will be okay. It's not in Kendall's interest to get any negative attention from us. I think she'd really like to hear about Alphonso. No hidden motive."

"Okay. Let me know how it went."

"I will. Thanks for your time."

After the workday, Kendall and I go home in our respective vehicles. I'll pick her up later.

In my apartment, I pick out a dress, then reconsider. I don't always dress up for a dinner at my parents', and I don't want to be obvious about my mixed emotions. Eventually, I go for slacks and a V-neck sweater, medium height pumps. Very little make-up. I'm not exactly sure what I want to convey, but tonight's conversation will have to be contained. It's my responsibility.

When I arrive at her condo, I realize Kendall had no such reservations.

"You look great," she says.

"That's nice of you to say. It's just dinner though. Nothing formal." She'll be a tad overdressed in the dark red dress with the matching pumps, but I can't seem to tear my gaze away.

"You don't like it?"

"I don't have time for this," I say, even though it's a message for me rather than for her. "Sorry, I didn't mean anything. Let's just do this, okay?"

"Whatever you like."

We're venturing into hazardous waters, and we're not even there yet.

Chapter Eight

A s a woman running a corporation, I'm aware that perception matters. The last time Blake, Robyn's father, saw me, I was in holding, awaiting my bail hearing.

Now I'm joining the family for dinner, wearing clothes that tell him, if nothing else, I'm back in charge.

I'm sort of dating his daughter. I'm sure he caught the fine print because his eyes widen when we walk in together. He's polite though.

"Kendall, welcome," he says. "I've looked through some old photos, and I think I found something interesting for you. I'll show you later."

"I'd love that. Thank you so much for having me."

"Well, we can't say no to Robyn," he deadpans.

I'm still reading the room. He and my father were apparently close at some point, close enough that he managed to insert himself in the organization—ironically, just like Robyn did. That's where the similarities end. In the present, Blake is friendly but cautious. I understand. As a Mancini, I know the importance of protecting myself just as my father did. We don't give up all our secrets that easily.

"I'm glad," I say while Robyn gives him a smile that's a bit terse.

Her mother Veronica shakes my hand. "How about we start with a cocktail? Dinner is almost ready."

I sure don't mind starting with a bit of alcohol. Robyn gives me a questioning look, and I hurry to say, "That would be great. And don't look so worried, I've been cutting down on the pain pills. I'm fine." The silence that ensues is a bit awkward, which I understand. We're talking life-changing events, life-or-death situations. Yes, I'd really like that cocktail now.

"Why don't you take a seat?" Veronica suggests. "We'll be right back."

Blake follows her into the kitchen, while I sit on the couch. Robyn hesitates and chooses an armchair.

"Relax a little," I say. "This is going fine, right? And you cleared family dinner with SAC Carr. We're good."

"Yeah." She nods. "Maybe I'm just too eager to expect bad things to happen."

"It's been rough, I'm the last person to dispute that. But we're fine here. Got to live a little."

Robyn laughs, shaking her head. "I think I need someone to pinch me. This is surreal."

"Hey, I didn't know you were into that, but I can help you. A little later, but still."

Yes, I definitely have things under control. I managed to get her all flustered in the time it took for the parents to bring the cocktails with a Campari-orange flavor.

The answers Blake might or might not have for me aren't the best dinner conversation though, and neither is Robyn's job, which was his job before he retired.

"This is very good," I say. "And I have to tell you, I like the surroundings much better than the last time we met."

This is for Blake who gives me a wry smile. "I can imagine. We're happy to have you."

"Thank you. You have a lovely home."

It seems like everyone around the table is taking a deep breath in relief. Yes, art and furniture make for a good subject for some small talk. Easy. Safe.

Blake takes his time. After dinner, he suggests, "How about we go to my office? We'll stick to the plan, of course. This is informal, but you might want to hear about this in private."

"Sure," I say, keeping the smile on my face. "The law forbids me to have any secrets from Robyn at this time, but I think we can work that out later. I'd love to see those pictures you mentioned."

"Great. We can have dessert and coffee after that."

Curious, I follow him to his office where we sit down. Blake picks up a box that contains photographs and takes out a few. My jaw drops a little at seeing the young boys in school uniforms.

"Yeah, that was a long time ago. We were over at each other's houses almost every day, really close, until we changed schools, and it got harder to keep in touch."

"You found each other again though."

"Yeah. We met a few times over the years."

I look at the black and white photograph again. "He trusted you enough to let you in, even when you didn't always have his best interests in mind." I'm not sure why this slipped out. Too much wine maybe. Or perhaps I resent him, like I still resent Robyn a little for crossing those lines. Myself, for letting them. I should have been around, picked up something that Jimmy and Luca apparently didn't, and perhaps Dad would still be alive.

"I'm not sure what the FBI, or your family told you, but I wasn't looking to set him up."

"Really?"

"I was trying to protect him, and Angela. I'm sorry I failed, Kendall. I'm deeply sorry about that, but not everything is how it seems."

"Okay. I should let you explain. Since I've been enjoying your hospitality, I think I owe you that much."

"I think you owe that to yourself more than anything. A lot of people have been telling a lot of stories lately, but this is what I know to be true: Al wanted to come clean. He wanted to run a legitimate business, and make sure you and Angela were protected. We were working on making that happen."

"But then Jimmy found out."

He sighs. "Al had a hard time believing that Jimmy might betray him. In the beginning, he had this idea that you two might get married, start a family. While your dad understood that it wasn't going to happen, Jimmy never did."

I sit back in my chair, recent conversations with Jimmy flashing on my mind.

"There's no point in beating yourself up," Blake says, reading my thoughts correctly. "He was a good actor."

"I guess so." I'm still absorbing the fact that Dad could be deeply involved in the FBI investigation, basically an informant? "So my father was willing to risk it all."

"Because he believed that his parents, and grandparents had gone astray to a certain extent. And he wanted a clean legacy for you, and the generations after that."

"Wow." That's not very eloquent, but I'm not sure what else there is to say.

"He was doing the right thing. So are you."

Whatever his approval is worth, I can't ignore that it feels good. Luca and Claudia, my closest family members, were a lot more critical this week, and in the recent past. I'll have to draw my own conclusions from that, see who really showed up for me. Sofia. Robyn and her family. It's a confusing upside-down world.

"Do you have any more questions? If not, we can go back down for that coffee and strawberry shortcake in a minute."

"Sounds great."

Before I have a chance to wonder what's going to happen in that minute, he continues, "Just one more thing. I swear this is the truth, and we were trying our best to help Al. No one is happier than me that the ones responsible for his death are finally held accountable. But whatever game it is you're playing with my daughter...stop."

"What...?"

"I think you heard me, Kendall."

Oh, I did. "With all due respect, you don't want to know about the games I'm playing with your daughter." I get to my feet. "Thank you for everything, Blake. I appreciate it more than you can imagine. Robyn is a grown woman, and so am I. Don't forget it. I'd love a piece of that cake now."

I leave the office, and he has no choice but to follow me back down.

This has been most enlightening.

Boundaries sufficiently established, and with less pain than any day since *that* day, I feel amazing. I feel like celebrating, even with the patronizing warning I received from Blake. I know his brand of mild-mannered machismo because Dad was the same. Nothing for me to worry about.

Robyn, unaware of the details of my conversation with her father, seems to have finally loosened up by the time we enjoy dessert with coffee.

"Everything has been delicious," I say. "Again, thank you so much. Frankly, for a long time I didn't know what would make a difference to my grief, but this has helped me. The conversations with all of you...and in my family, we say that excellent food cures everything. I think that's very true."

Veronica looks pleased, Blake a tad resigned. Nevertheless, he's been a good sport.

"Let's drink to that," he says. "If you have room for a small digestif?"

For a second, I think Robyn will decline the offer, but instead she shrugs.

"I think we do."

A home-cooked meal with the Johnsons, it's almost as good as an evening at *Catania*. When family matters, it shows. This evening has given me a lot to think about.

An hour later, we walk through the front door of my condo.

"This wasn't just about a few old photos and stories, was it?"

I won't insult Robyn's intelligence by telling her she's wrong.

"You nailed it. It seems like Dad was about to be an informant which is something to wrap my head around, still. Blake was very friendly and polite except he warned me to keep my hands off you."

Her expression clearly shows her disapproval. "He said that?"

"Not in those exact words, but yes. I might have responded with something resembling sexual innuendo."

"I don't know what to say to that. But every time you open your mouth, it's something resembling sexual innuendo, and to be honest, I'm tired of it."

That sounds harsh, I was going to say, but the next moment, her mouth is on mine, her kiss demanding. Robyn steps back and elaborates, "The innuendo part, that is."

"Yeah, I got it. Does that mean you're going to stay over again?"

"How much more bizarre can this day get?" she wonders out loud.

I pull her close for another kiss, let my hand wander over her shoulder, down her back and then let it slide past the waistband of her slacks. She gasps in surprise.

"Nothing bizarre about this," I whisper. Her slacks fall to the floor, and she steps out of them. Her sweater is next, and she's standing in front of me in nothing but her underwear. "Let's go somewhere more comfortable."

"You don't want to undress?"

"It can wait a little." I love how that…innuendo…makes her eyes darken with desire. "I missed you."

"I missed you too," she admits. In the bedroom, I finally get her all naked. I get out of my dress, but leave the bra and panties for the moment, give her a light push, and climb in bed with her. I'm not completely pain-free yet, but it's mild enough to ignore.

It's a rushed, impatient encounter as we're both aware we're on borrowed time, always have been. But it's so worth it, having her under my hands, in my hands, stifling her moans with deep kisses. This is not about controlling anything, on her side or mine. This is happening because we want it.

Robyn doesn't take more than a few seconds to relax. She's all over me, mindful of recent injuries, but not shy. My panties sail to the floor, and her hands, warm and confident, open me to her as she gets comfortable. She leans in for a taste, and the world is vanishing in a haze of pleasure. Being with her like this is safe. I close my eyes, shivering under her touch, her hair tickling my thighs until the sensations take me over. I don't try to prolong the inevitable.

I can finally let go.

Chapter Nine

"That was intense," I observe. In the mirror on the other side of the room, I can see my own somewhat stunned expression, my disheveled hair. Kendall is only now removing her bra. Seeing her wince, I hurry to help.

"Thanks. And yes," she rasps. "Intense."

Whatever that means, this had nothing to do with my initial undercover assignment, or the case. I've come to think that it was unavoidable, and her constant teasing of me was only partly to blame.

I wanted her.

I want her.

It makes no difference who I pretend to be—this hasn't changed. The depth of the sexual attraction between us still surprises me. Is it that continued aspect of danger and taboo? I don't know. All I know is that looking at her now, comfortable and naked, I want to touch her again. Judging from her smile, it's not that hard to decipher what's on my mind.

"Don't overthink it," Kendall says. She sounds amused.

"I need to think about it a little. Perhaps I should send Ryan to go to work with you. It might be the best solution for everyone."

"I like it better to have you at work with me. What's the problem? The numbers don't lie. It's not like you're going to misinterpret them because I gave you great orgasms."

I have to laugh at that though I can't deny the fact.

"I'm serious, okay? It's more her expertise anyway."

"Anything about my business is your expertise now. At some point, the IRS folks will take over anyway."

I see I'm getting nowhere with this. I will have to make some decisions. If I go there, I'll have to have some uncomfortable and overdue conversations. Kendall's family knows. Dad picked up on things from one evening—I guess Kendall dressing up for the occasion didn't help.

With sudden dread I realize that this, I cannot explain away, to me, or anyone. Undercover, I needed to do what I had to so she wouldn't suspect anything. To get close to her.

But Kendall Mancini knows who I am.

"Relax," she says. "Please. I know we'll still have to figure out some things, but we'll do it together, okay? We're both here, alive. And this was some of the best sex I've had in my life. All of that counts for something."

"And what is that?" I can't help myself, scooting closer, and she reaches out for me.

"I'm not sure exactly, but just to be on the safe side, let's give it another try."

I can't say no.

"You look awfully tense," she observes when we have breakfast on the rooftop terrace the next morning. The city's just now waking up. We still have some time before we have to make decisions—again.

"You think? That's not the nicest thing to say after last night."

"I'm just wondering what you're still worried about, after last night."

There's not a hint of teasing in her tone. I guess I owe her a real answer then.

"After today, I'll have to talk to Ryan. I have to talk to SAC Carr anyway, because of the dinner with my parents..."

Kendall shrugs. "We had great food and wine. Your Dad showed me pictures from when he and my dad were boys. And he said that Dad was all in. It looks like I'd have his approval for wanting a clean slate so that's what we're doing. I don't know why we need to involve Agent Farmer."

"Because she's not sleeping with you?" I'm not sure how much clearer I could be about making my point.

"That's right, she's not. As far as I know, she has a wife and a baby."

Kendall never ceases to catch me off guard. Ryan is a very private person. I don't know her well.

"How did you know?"

She looks at me like I asked something dense, and she doesn't know how to phrase that in polite terms.

"Habit, I guess. I like to know whom I'm dealing with, always have. I could still kick myself over not seeing the signs with Jimmy. Perhaps I was fooling myself thinking I could channel his obsession with me into an acceptable work ethic, but when you showed me the money he embezzled that was pretty much out of the window."

I hold her gaze, wondering if I need to ask the question.

Kendall laughs. "You know my business, and you know the people around me. You really think I have some private militia I'd sic on investigators and prosecutors? Life is too short."

We have created a fragile peace, or at least a ceasefire between us. I might be about to blow it.

"To your knowledge, did your father ever do anything like that? Try to get a case against someone thrown out, threaten retribution?"

"I understand you wouldn't ask the question if you didn't already know the answer. I'm not naïve. That probably happened, though I wasn't ever a witness to it. Why does this matter anyway? He's dead."

"Yes. I'm sorry."

I'm still trying to wrap my head around Al Mancini being one of the "almost" good guys. I guess she is too.

"I don't want to cause you any trouble," Kendall says. "But I don't think we need to change anything. I have not asked you to change any numbers, or to hold anything back from your employer, have I?"

"No," I admit.

"You've been enjoying yourself?" Her smile tells me that she, too, doesn't ask questions to which she doesn't already know the answer. "Then everything is fine."

What if I allowed myself to believe this?

What if?

"I wish this case was over."

My exclamation elicits a sigh from her, and her tone is unusually sober.

"Me too," she says.

It's a little more complicated than that. I report to SAC Carr later that day.

"Given what I've learned, which isn't that much, I thought I should study up on Alphonso Mancini's case a bit more. According to my father, he was going to work with the authorities so his family would be safe from both the Biancos, and possible prosecution. I think there's more to learn for us."

"That makes sense," she agrees. "Kendall might have some more information if you manage to jog her memory, and that could help strengthen the case against other members of the Bianco family, and the Rossis. If you need any other resources, let me know."

"There is something I was thinking of...If Agent Farmer could be available to help with the daily checks. I understand the Mancini's business pretty well, but she'd see red flags right away."

"So do you, I think," Carr says. I'm not sure what that frown means. "Sure, talk to Agent Farmer, and maybe get someone on those old files, see if anything stands out. Otherwise, I want you to stay close to Kendall. You've formed a rapport. She trusts you."

This is wrong on so many levels, and there are many things I could say. For example, it's unethical, because I'm falling for her a little bit more whenever I spend time with her. We've formed a rapport all right, a highly sensual and sexual one. Even here at the office with my supervisor, the thought causes an inappropriate pang of desire. I can't give this up.

I can't give up my job. There will be other assignments, right? Bad people to go after, with no blurred lines? Once I'm there, what else is going to happen? I'll still see Kendall?

Oh my God. The chaos has not dissipated one bit, and I don't know that it ever will.

"Is there anything else?"

"No. Thank you. I'll meet with Agent Farmer."

"You do that. Have a good evening."

We'll see.

I catch Ryan on her way out. I can't blame her for being cautious, if not suspicious, around me.

"You want me to come look over Mancini's shoulder with you?" she asks. "I thought it was clear that you didn't need me on the case."

"I talked it over with SAC Carr, and she agrees. I'm going to need more resources."

"It's probably not the worst gig." She shrugs. "I hear she's giving out free pizza and wine. That's a bit iffy regarding ethics, but they say *Catania* is the best place in town for this kind of food."

"Oh, it's good," I say, my cheeks warming.

"I guess it's okay as long as we keep the receipts. So, tell me, you think she's complying so far?"

"From what I've seen, yes. She wants to get this over with as much as we do."

"Second chances, huh? You think someone like her deserves them?"

"It's not about deserving, but the framework the law gives us. Her father wanted to come clean before he was murdered, and now she's been helping us with the Biancos and their connections. I'd say that works."

"Looks like it. All right, I'll see you tomorrow then?"

"What about tonight, how about we do have dinner and hash this out some more?"

She gives me a wry smile.

"At *Catania*?"

Before I can answer, my phone rings. It's Kendall.

"I'm sorry, I have to take this."

"Hey beautiful," she says, and I turn away from Ryan's scrutiny so fast I can feel the whiplash.

"I'm still at work, but perhaps you could reserve a table for two at *Catania*?"

"I like the sound of that," Kendall says. "I've been thinking of you all day."

"I was with you most of the day. This is for work too. I'm bringing a colleague..." I lower my voice. "Sorry about that."

"I see. You already have your plus one. How about a table for three?"

"I'm not sure if that's a good idea."

"I am. I'd like to talk to Agent Farmer as well. See you there in half an hour."

"Kendall..." I say, but she's already ended the call. I turn back to Ryan whose poker face can't quite hide her curiosity.

"*Catania* it is," I say. "And we'll definitely keep the receipts."

—ele—

Much to her credit, Kendall has a table ready for us in the familiar area, but she leaves me and Ryan to discuss the specifics over an appetizer platter before she comes to sit with us.

"Agent Farmer, it's nice to see you again."

It occurs to me I long for a world in which I wouldn't have to look over my shoulder. As a lesbian. A woman in a male-dominated field. Sharing a bed with Kendall Mancini.

I wonder if Ryan has some of the same thoughts, minus waking sex dreams of Kendall, of course. I hope.

"Be careful what you wish for," Ryan counters. "It looks like you're going to see a lot more of me in the future."

"Oh well, this too shall pass." They both laugh, and I feel like I've been catapulted into an alternate universe. Was there anything funny about this?

"It will," Ryan agrees.

"Good. In the meantime, there's no reason we can't enjoy the good things nature has to offer us." That particular smile is for me only, and it makes me squirm a bit. Perhaps that's her punishing me for bringing my work, and colleague, to this place. Again.

Ryan accepts a main course, coffee, and dessert, but she shakes her head when Kendall offers her wine.

"No problem. Just let me know if you'd like anything other than water and coffee."

"I'm fine, thanks."

Again, I have the odd feeling that I might have missed something.

Chapter Ten

T hings are going well so far. Under control. I don't like that Agent Farmer will be a regular for the next few weeks, but only because it limits my ability to flirt with Robyn on the job.

I continue to do what I signed up for, be transparent about the day-to-day business.

I also know that Ryan once had an inappropriate relationship with a therapist—inappropriate on the therapist's side who has long since lost her license. Ryan's wife stood by her. Ryan had also been twenty years sober prior to the relationship and is apparently doing well now.

In my business, I have to know my friends and my enemies, and all the shades of gray in between.

Luca shows up at the end of the day, nervous. He's always nervous these days. We found a buyer for Adria, and he doesn't like it. I hope with the date getting closer, he'll tell me more.

"It's not going to happen before the first of the month, right?"

"Don't worry," I assure him. "We've set the meeting for the eighth. What is so important about a few days?"

"I have some business to wrap up. I can't do it all at *Catania*."

"How about doing it in actual business space?" I suggest, not even trying to be sarcastic about it. We have some of the best space in town.

Luca shakes his head, giving me a frustrated sigh. "Sometimes I don't know if you're just that naïve, or if you're trying to annoy me. Remember when we first got involved in Adria?"

"Oh, I do. No one really wanted to, but for the sake of our elders, we had to keep it going at least."

"Yeah. At any cost. And not all talents of our elders were with gourmet food. Kendall, I've been scrambling to keep all the suppliers up to date and pay everyone what they are owed. This is the ugly part that my father had to deal with because yours wanted to keep his hands clean."

"Wait a minute. What the hell are you talking about?" I don't have to work hard to muster the anger. This has been going on far too long, under my nose, because Uncle Lorenzo was a homophobe using bigotry to keep Luca in line. Everyone kept harping on how I should marry Bruno so a man could hold the reins. This is so fucked up.

"So, when are you planning to do this 'wrapping up'?" I ask. "And don't get me wrong, I don't need to know details. I just don't want our legitimate business partners to run into people you still have to pay."

"It's all so easy for you, isn't it?" he sneers.

"Hey, easy. If it wasn't for me, and Agent Johnson, you wouldn't be here doing any business at all."

"You're threatening me?"

"I'm telling it to you like it is. We're running a clean business. If Uncle Lorenzo, may he rest in peace, was running drugs, that's over now. And we won't have any of that homophobic, sexist BS creep into day-to-day operations either."

"You're talking about my father," he says, indignant.

"Yes, your father who scared you into teaming up with Jimmy to beat up a woman and God knows what else. You want to tell me that's not disgusting, because it includes family? I'm not scared to put a name to it."

"You always had it too easy."

"You said that already. Yes, perhaps it was easier for me, but here we are. My buyers will be there on the eighth, and we'll all sign the contract. So, when is that other thing of yours going down?"

"You don't have to worry about that. We'll just have a quick meeting Friday night, after we close. Last delivery, last payment."

"Delivery." I frown. "You have buyers?"

"Yeah, that's all lined up, but it doesn't have anything to do with Adria, or the Mancini Group, I swear."

"You better. You know I have those ladies from the FBI all over me."

"I can only imagine."

Of course, he felt the need to sneak an almost slur into this.

"It will be all right. After that we can talk about what you want to do next. I could buy you out if you prefer that."

"You brought the FBI into the house, and you want to kick me out?"

"Like I said, we'll talk later, after all those deals have gone through. You should go home."

Luca gets to his feet, but he still has to argue, raising an index finger to my face as he speaks.

"This is not what our fathers had in mind. This is not bringing honor to the family, it's destroying it."

I sit still, regarding him.

"You know it," he insists.

"You sound like a Bianco," I finally say. "I go to work every freaking day and run a multi-billion-dollar business. You wanted to get rich quick using Adria for drug deals or whatever it is you've got going on, and you think that's honorable?"

"Dream on, Kendall," he says, his contempt obvious.

I jump a bit when he slams the door, though it's rather predictable. Waiting, I move a stack of paperclips back and forth, then start to arrange them in a pattern. A rectangle. A heart.

A few minutes later, Robyn comes in with Farmer. I close the blinds to make sure no one can see inside the office from the hallway and start to unbutton my blouse. I didn't need to do it here and now, but the way Robyn's eyes widen is too sweet.

"Okay, ladies," I say. "How did I do?"

"How did I do?" I ask her again, later, in a much different context. Robyn clearly makes the connection to when she and Farmer came to collect the wire I was wearing for my conversation with Luca. I can tell from the flash of impatience on her face. It's gone in a heartbeat, because the answer is the same this time, and I know it.

Her face is flushed, and she's still breathless. So beautiful.

"I think you could tell."

I reach out to touch her side, letting me hand wander to her hips and down between her thighs. Robyn draws a sharp breath at the slightest of pressure.

"I think I still can. You know," I say, holding her gaze, "it might not be the worst idea to bring another agent into this."

"I don't want to talk about Ryan right now." Her words come out in a moan.

"I understand. Sorry. You are my priority."

My actions underline the truth of my statement.

"I like that," she whispers.

"I know you do. Just this one thing—once this is all over, I'd like us to go on a little getaway."

My own breath catches in my throat. I love this deep sensual connection, when the minute movement of fingertips creates a world of desire.

"Because that went so well the last time?"

"It will be perfect this time," I promise, leaning in to kiss her, and then I pull her close, the shiver running through her body almost setting off the fireworks in mine. We make a pretty good team in everything.

Chapter Eleven

I don't have much time to think about a possible get-away. We are almost about to wrap up our time at the Mancini Group. Next, the focus will on Luca Mancini and shutting down the drug deals he's apparently been making from Adria.

Kendall has been recording their conversations for a while. After finding something alarming, she agreed to wear a wire. She'll try to make peace in the next few days, perhaps get invited to the meeting. For all his bluster, Luca is in over his head.

I thought we were in a good place, but my bubble is burst when Ryan finds me in the break room, looking...shocked? Angry? I'm not quite sure. She doesn't waste time either.

"What does she have over you?"

"Excuse me?"

"You know exactly what I'm talking about. You've built a rapport with her all right. You seem to forget this is a job."

"I know it is. What is your problem? We got Luca Mancini on record admitting he's dealing drugs out of the restaurant. We'll be able to bust him and his part-ners."

"Kendall seems to think you're her friend. When someone like her makes that assessment, it means something."

"It means that we're transparent with each other. Come on, you don't think—" I stop it right there, because most of what she might be assuming, is true.

"Think what? That you're sleeping with her? It's pretty obvious to me."

"Ryan. No."

"If I can tell, others will too. Is this why you wanted me on the case?"

"You got this all wrong. We need this bust to happen, and after that, her case is in the hands of the IRS or whoever wants their share. I wanted your help so we could move faster. It's happening, and I'm glad about it. Kendall saved my life, risking more legal trouble for herself. I can appreciate that, okay? She almost got herself killed getting me out."

"Yeah, I remember that."

I can tell she's not entirely convinced. I have to think of what Kendall told me about knowing who you do business with. I know that Ryan left the FBI for a while, then came back about a couple of years ago. She has her own set of secrets, though I might be acting petty and defensive. She might have better reasons.

"Let's get this over with, okay? I swear she doesn't have anything over me."

That is almost true. We're past the point where she could use our relationship as leverage. It's not in Kendall's interest to create a situation that ends both of our careers and livelihoods—or where we could never see each other again.

"You two are acting like you're close. If you don't want anyone to get that impression—" I note how she doesn't say, "the wrong impression." "You should be more careful."

"I'll keep that in mind. Thank you."

Hoping I avoided the worst, I carry my coffee and snack back to my desk and sit with a sigh of relief. This will work. For now. After the bust, the premise will change. I don't work for the IRS, and if Kendall continues to be transparent and works with them, my job will be done.

For a moment, I daydream about evenings at *Catania*, and nights at her condo without the guilt.

It's a short moment. My phone rings, and I pick up.

"Robyn," my father says. "Do you have a minute?"

I look at the papers related to some of Al Mancini's old business deals and decide I do.

"Yes. Is everything okay with you and Mom?" We haven't talked since I brought the former head of a crime family to dinner. Or is it the head of a former crime family?

"Yes, of course. Could we meet?"

That sounds serious, like it's something he can't tell me on the phone. "I still have some work to do, but I could sneak out for a coffee in a couple of hours. Can it wait that long?"

"I'll see you then."

It's with a sense of trepidation that I walk into the coffee shop. I don't care for getting yelled at again, especially not by Dad who used his friendship with Al Mancini to try and get him to turn himself in. Lines were crossed long before I graduated.

To my surprise, Dad hugs me with a smile. This might not be an awkward uncomfortable conversation. Maybe it's about planning Mom's birthday party?

Once we both have a coffee and pastry in front of us, he quickly disavows me of that notion.

"It's about Kendall," he says.

I can't help the sigh. "There I thought we were planning Mom's birthday."

"We can talk about that, too, but this is something I thought you should know."

At least, it doesn't seem that urgent?

"I'm so ready for this case to come to a close, but...I'm listening."

"I haven't thought about this in a long time," he says. "It's nowhere in the records, and it might be nothing. Or a figure of speech."

"I assume you're going to give me something more specific?"

"You think Kendall is honest about her business?"

"I shouldn't be discussing this with you, but yes, she is. I have proof."

She's been hesitant to go against family, but still she's delivering Luca and the dirty money in Adria to us—even knowing that the sale might be in serious jeopardy.

"Good. All right, here's something Al talked about every once in a while, a 'college fund' he had for Kendall."

"College?" I repeat, puzzled. "By the time you went undercover, she had long graduated and taken on a role in the company."

"This is why I assumed it was some sort of metaphor or code."

"What does it mean?"

"I never found out, but I'm pretty sure Al was planning ahead. Whatever happened with the business, and the family, he wanted Kendall to be all right."

"Given the amounts of money this family is moving around, 'all right' is relative."

"It is," Dad agrees. "This is why I wanted to come to you first. Make some inquires, figure out if Kendall knows about this. If she's holding anything back right now, that could come back to haunt her."

"You're trying to protect me, or her?" I ask, my tone more serious than I intended. Dad didn't take it as a joke either.

"I got the impression that protecting her would serve you too."

I drink my coffee, stalling, but perhaps he doesn't expect a confession or denial.

"Kendall loves the business. She never asked for any of the other stuff."

He acknowledges that with a shrug. "Perhaps, but the other stuff is part of what gave her this business, and her wealth. There has to be some sort of accountability."

"Would Alphonso have gotten off without a prison sentence?"

Would you have done whatever you could to make that happen?

"I don't know for sure," Dad admits. "That was certainly the plan, get him into the witness protection program."

"Just him?"

"Angela and Kendall as well, if it had come to that."

I mull that over. "So, you think Al had some money stashed away for emergencies of any kind?"

"Something like that, but he was very vague about it. He was going to tell me more once we had worked out a deal on paper. Of course, that never happened."

"I'll look into it," I say. "You're right. If Kendall's keeping any secrets at this point, this will be endless. And she might go to prison after all."

I didn't realize how worried I was about that prospect until I catch his gaze.

"Dad. Thank you for telling me."

"You'll do the right thing."

"Yes, I will."

I was going to spend the night at home, but this is more urgent, isn't it?

———ele———

"I was hoping you'd come by," Kendall says, pleased, when she opens the door to me. "Are you hungry? We could order in, or maybe swing by Adria for one last time? Come to think of it, I might feel like going somewhere that's not associated with the family, in a good or a bad way. Let's go for some Thai."

"Kendall. We need to talk."

"Right now? What's the dimension of this talk? Something that came up, or the general state of...everything?"

I step into her personal space and kiss her. Stalling, perhaps, and because I can't help it. I love the instant, inevitable intimacy between us, the way my body craves her touch. I force myself to step back.

"Okay. I like the way you start a conversation."

"When will you understand that I'm trying to help you?" I stop myself short of using a swear word, but even so, the sentiment comes across.

"Sit down. Please. Care to tell me what this is about?"

"Your father talked to mine about a college fund he had set aside for you."

I can see nothing but confusion in her gaze. "This is what got you upset? I assumed your parents did the same at the time, and please, don't ask me where the money came from. I was not privy to all the business secrets back then."

"That's exactly what this is about, the secrets you were privy to. It wasn't a real college fund, just code for something else, and it was done more recently. A back-up plan if you want, for whatever was going to happen once he started cooperating."

"Look, Robyn, I can't tell you what they were talking about. I was busy at the time, and I didn't go home all that often. But this is the first time I'm hearing about it."

"You're telling the truth?"

"I swear. I'll admit that I lied to you before, but not since Bianco took you. That whole story with Luca, it's not easy for me. I knew Uncle Lorenzo wasn't as pure as the driven snow, but I didn't know he was that dirty. I sure as hell didn't think Luca would jump in with both feet."

"I understand." I hold her gaze, trying to figure out if I can trust my instincts. Still. "I have to be sure that you're not withholding anything else. This is serious."

"I'm not. This makes no sense to me anyway. Dad knew I was going to run the company and do it successfully. I never talked to him about children either. There was no need for a college fund, metaphorically and literally."

"All right." I take a deep breath, but the relief doesn't come yet. "I suppose you could interest me in Thai food. I've thrived on caffeine and sweet snacks today."

"Good. I know a place."

"Your car or mine?"

"Neither. We can walk from here."

True to her promise, it's less than a five-minute walk in the balmy night air. It's strange, or at least should be, how natural this feels. Going out for dinner with my...what could I call her without exaggerating? We're still in limbo. Part of me is afraid we'll always be, that I'll wake up someday with nothing but regrets.

Today is not that day.

Kendall has been here before. We are shown to a table by a huge window, and the waiter brings leather-bound menus. I'll pay for my food, but this isn't something I can write off for expenses. After we've made our orders, I lean back into the booth and study her.

"You like what you see?"

We've made progress. Now she's teasing me in private only. And, yes, I do.

"I've been thinking about that getaway you proposed. How would that even work? You surrendered your passport."

"So I can't go on a commercial flight, and we need to stay inside the country. So far, not a problem."

"Except for...the appearance of impropriety?"

She laughs as she picks up her glass. "I thought we were truly past that. Would you prefer it if I asked you to marry me?"

I can't ignore it, my heart is starting to hammer.

"Come on. Don't be ridiculous."

She doesn't answer right away, but still wears that enigmatic smile.

"Have you dated anyone since you were Jessica Byrne?" she asks, referring to the name of my undercover persona. It seems ages ago that I used it.

"No," I confess.

"Me neither. I'd say that's a good start."

"To think about marriage?"

"To think about all kinds of options. Once this is over, would you like to...explore some of them?"

Like everything about Kendall, this seems far too easy and tempting. We still have to hide our relationship, yet she's talking like there are no boundaries ever—about marriage, and grandchildren. I'm living a bizarre dream that hovers between pleasant and dangerous. It has been both. One can change to the other at any given moment.

"At some point, yes. But I can't go anywhere with you right now. After that deal..."

"You mean after you'll arrest my cousin."

"We kept him out of jail for as long as we could, but that was before he talked about meeting with drug runners at one of your restaurants."

"You have a point," she admits with a sigh. "But you didn't really answer my question."

"Tell me a bit more. Where would we go? Your real estate includes hotels I assume? Or somewhere more private? Because I'm telling you I'm not going back to the cabin."

"I assumed you'd say that. And I agree with you that after the cloak and dagger stuff is done would be better timing. I want it to be a surprise."

"Well, as long as there are no surprises with Luca..."

"There won't be. I swear. Believe me, I can't wait to get rid of Adria."

"Even if part of it might go to the government?"

"Can't be worse than it is now, right?" She's aware that I'm still testing her. It will be a while before I can truly stop that.

I want the whole truth. Given how I've handled the conversations with Ryan and my dad today, I don't have a lot of room to talk.

"So," I say, "how are you planning on proposing?"

"If I told you, that would take away all the suspense, wouldn't it?"

She's still one step ahead. But the meal and wine—and company—are too good to complain.

Chapter Twelve

Nothing is ever that easy, right? I remember the dead rat, delivered to me in holding while I was waiting for my bail hearing. That was Bianco's doing, and he has nothing to do with Luca's shady deals, but still. I might have a target on my back, and the same could go for Robyn. There's never a bad time to look over your shoulder.

Better be paranoid than dead. Those are dark thoughts after a promising evening spent with her, once again, because she couldn't wait until tomorrow to ask me about Blake's vague hunch.

Maybe I am paranoid. Nothing happens on our way back, the air filled with opportunity more than insinuation. Robyn left some doors open—and I'm pretty sure we'll have the opportunity soon. My attorneys have assured me that the FBI investigation will be coming to a close, especially with Luca behaving badly.

Then, Robyn and I might have to make a few decisions, which, I think is best done in beautiful surroundings.

"Thank you, this was great," she said. "Another recommendation I'll have to keep in mind."

"We can come back whenever you like. Getting food is not inappropriate in any way...Though I do enjoy the inappropriate things as well."

"I should go home."

"If you prefer. Come up for a little nightcap? I can have the driver take you home, in your car if you like."

After a moment of hesitation, Robyn agrees. We step into the elevator, each hanging on to our own thoughts. Would Dad have been ready to give up Uncle Lorenzo?

We all try to protect those closest to us. Bad decisions have consequences. At this point, few people are closer to me than the woman by my side. The irony.

It's still warm outside, so we have a drink on the rooftop terrace. The glass panes give us shelter from the wind, but don't obstruct the amazing view. I felt like champagne. Robyn laughs at that, but she doesn't say no.

"Would you miss it?" she asks.

"What do you mean? This place? I could live somewhere else. It just needs to be in the city. I wanted to impress you with the cabin, but honestly that place gives me the creeps now."

"The luxury," she says. "Dining at all those restaurants, living in a place like this...I know that when we close the case, the IRS will have more questions. We don't know yet what they will impose."

"I survived Bianco. I think I can survive whatever they throw at me." After all, there's the "college fund." I didn't lie to Robyn, not all the way, that is. It might be an urban legend, but now that she has reminded me it might be worth looking into, just to be sure. "To answer the question—yes. A person can get used to this, and I'm not looking into downsizing too much. I have the hope that you guys will write me a letter of recommendation for being such a good girl and complying." I give her a look, long enough to make her flustered. "You like it too."

"Who wouldn't?" At least she's not trying to deny it. I get rather impatient when people are in denial about this. Money doesn't solve all problems. It does have a way of easing your mind, even now when I know the final verdict will hurt.

I have heard people talk about money, somewhere, they didn't know exactly where, that my father set aside for emergencies. I always assumed it was included in my inheritance, that it had no special designation. No secrecy. I might be wrong.

"Right? Look, I know this might go either way, but I'm trying to keep it together for now. We've had a lot of shockwaves in this family, and we're heading towards another one."

"You are doing the right thing."

"I know. I'm not worried at this point." Even as I say it, I feel the shiver skitter down my spine. Nothing is ever completely settled. I have enemies, for being a woman running a successful corporation, for being a Mancini. The Biancos are busy saving their hides right now, but they won't forget I shot Tony.

Claudia and Elena, and other family members will be truly pissed at me come next week, though I doubt they'll declare a vendetta. And then there are Luca's nebulous business contacts, likely high-profile drug dealers that frequent Adria. Come to think of it, I have a lot of reasons to be worried, even with Tony dead, and Jimmy Bruno behind bars. I'll definitely look into that "college fund."

"Would you mind if I stayed and we just...slept?" she asks. "I'd love to do more, but I'm really tired."

"That's okay, of course."

My future plans, one way or another, will include her. It's not just for romantic reasons though they definitely play a role. For both of our safety, it's best that we stick together.

That night, it takes me a long time to fall asleep as I alternately wonder where to start looking for that fund without raising red flags, and what unpleasant surprises the future might hold. Next to me, Robyn seems to have no such problems. Snuggled in my arms, she's sleeping soundly.

The warmth of her body and her calm breathing finally lure me into sleep too. The awakening is...not rude, but reason for concern. At first, I'm not sure what woke me, but the various sounds that follow, rustling, footsteps, the lock in the door, are a dead giveaway.

I realize that Robyn is already out of bed, wearing PJ bottoms and a tank top. She's holding a gun.

"You stay here."

"You've got to be kidding me," I mutter before I get my own gun from the drawer of the nightstand. Robyn doesn't blink, but she tells me in a clear hand gesture to stay behind.

When we enter the living area, it's pretty clear what I already assumed: They're gone.

"Don't touch anything," Robyn warns. She heads for the other rooms and returns after a quick search.

I'm still looking at the item on the floor, tempted to pick it up, but I know it's better to have her get it to their lab and tested for prints. Not that I think there are any.

No, it's not a rat this time.

No, I wasn't paranoid.

Someone was in my condo, made it past the state-of-the-art security system, and if they're sophisticated enough to do that, they sure as hell didn't leave any prints.

Turning around, I can see that Robyn is on the phone.

"What are you doing?"

"What do you think? We can't just ignore this. I need to get my team in here."

I take another look at the threat that the unwelcome visitor dropped off.

"Can't you just take it to the lab?"

"No, it's not that easy. You really think this has nothing to do with Luca's deal?"

"It could have to do with many things and people," I offer, realizing it's not the right thing to say when she shakes her head.

"Yes, right away," she says to the person on the other end of the call. "I'll see you then."

I really don't like it when decisions are taken out of my hands like that.

"We should get dressed," Robyn says, sounding apologetic now, and I can't argue with that either.

I am dressed now, but still uncomfortable with this many people in my space. Recent experiences, grief, betrayal, and detention have made me more protective of my privacy.

"And you called Agent Johnson right away?" SAC Carr asks. She's here, Hampton McKay is, there's no doubt they're taking this seriously.

The picture showing me and my parents, everyone's faces crossed out with a black marker, is on the way to the lab. A crime scene unit is examining the place for clues on how the offender got in.

"Yes. I knew I couldn't touch anything." I cast a look at Robyn who looks pensive. She's probably wondering how many lies, big and small, we'll have to tell tonight, and how they will affect the future.

"We had dinner tonight," she says. "I had some additional questions, and we discussed them over food." I assume they won't look at street cameras to determine that she never drove home? This can't be priority.

"I have a meeting with Luca tomorrow. You still want me to ask him to let me join the meeting?" I ask.

"Yes, we stick to the plan," Carr decides. "Agent Johnson, I want you to stay here, just in case."

"I have security staff," I feel the need to insert.

"Yes, and this person made it past them."

"Agent Johnson is going to be my live-in bodyguard?"

"She'll stay with you until we figure out how he got in." I swear SAC Carr is amused despite the circumstances. I can read her fairly well. She probably thinks I'm still bluffing, just like Hampton.

Robyn knows I'm not.

"Perhaps it would be a good idea to pack up and go to a hotel," she suggests. "I don't suppose he's coming back, but if the security system was compromised, we're too exposed here. We'll see after the meeting."

"I agree with Agent Johnson. Of course I'll pay for it. I have no desire for a repeat of last night. That part, anyway."

Carr raises an eyebrow, but she doesn't comment.

"Okay, why don't you start packing? You can swing by Agent Johnson's home afterwards, but don't tell anyone, not even your family or security staff."

"You don't have to tell me twice. This was an inside job. I'm more than happy to remove myself and Agent Johnson from the crosshairs for the foreseeable future."

"We're grateful for that, Ms. Mancini. Thank you."

I head to my bedroom and quickly pack a few clothes and toiletries for a few days' stay. The small sound from the doorway makes me look up, and I see it's Hampton who's not trying to back away. His frown is telling.

"You don't agree with your boss's decision?"

"Oh, you need to be careful, that's for sure. You've made a lot of enemies only in the past few months."

"Thanks so much, Agent McKay. I'm aware."

"Robyn cares about you. Don't let her down."

Before I can argue, he's gone from my line of vision, and I hear him talking to one of the tech people.

I finish packing, including one of the most important items. I don't plan on letting her down, now or ever. It looks like we're going to have a little getaway anyway, but I was right:

Nothing is settled.

I still need to find out about that mysterious fund.

⁓

First, we are getting settled in the hotel after Robyn had the chance to get some of her own clothes. I don't tell her about McKay's warning. I'm not entirely sure if he's being patronizing, or if he's aware. He doesn't seem eager to rat her out, so we'll proceed as planned.

After we get the keys and code for the Paradise Suite, Robyn once more checks the perimeter. Finally, she leans against the doorway to the bathroom, and sighs.

"Tired?" I ask. "It's still early. We can have breakfast delivered."

"No. I was just wondering when we can get into that hot tub."

Despite the challenging circumstances, I feel the smile form on my face.

"I need to work today which means you do, too...but I think tonight is a realistic prospect. Let's get some coffee first?"

"Yeah. Let's start with that."

Chapter Thirteen

I f we had any illusions about the coming meeting between Luca Mancini and the drug runners he's been
working with, they're all gone. This isn't going to be
quick or easy. Someone found out. Going through with
the meeting is risky, but I agree with SAC Carr. If Kendall
backs out now, it might be even more dangerous.

We'll have to wait for news from the lab, and in the
meantime...stay under the radar. Life in Kendall Mancini's orbit never ceases to feel strange and intriguing at
the same time.

The breakfast is luxurious, a generous mix of Amer-
ican and continental. I checked with the kitchen
first—no more surprises—and after being cleared,
Kendall ordered the brunch for two. I didn't think I
could sit down long enough, or have the appetite, but
apparently, I was wrong.

"Tell me your theory," she says. "Frank Bianco direct-
ing this crap from behind bars? Or Jimmy?"

"I'm not sure. That would be quite obvious."

"They're men," she says. "I've never known them to be
subtle."

She has a point.

"What about Luca? It seems like he's been doing this
for a while. You think other than Lorenzo maybe, other
family members knew, profited from that side business?"

Kendall considers this, but she shakes her head. "I can't say. I wish I was more certain, but at this point...I think Lorenzo was always vying for the #1 spot, and he was grooming Luca to be next. So maybe they had an agenda, especially after my parents died. Their bad luck that Jimmy was already on Bianco's payroll."

She sounds bitter, and I can't blame her. It occurs to me that one of the reasons we still have that rapport is that people who have been close to her, for much longer, betrayed her. I was just doing my job.

Yeah, right. I suppress a sigh. Up until a certain moment that's now hard to define.

"Okay. Let's talk about the meeting. I want you to be careful. Don't draw attention to yourself."

"You're going to give me a safe word?" she asks, and suddenly it doesn't sound like it's something we could do in public.

"I'm not sure I'd call it a safe word. That would be for other occasions." Two can play that game.

She acknowledges my retort with a smile.

Time to get serious.

We get ready and drive to the company where we are going over more details of the meeting. The people coming to see Luca know who Kendall is, and that she's about to sell Adria. Other than that...I'd prefer if she stayed mostly quiet until we move in.

A part of me doesn't like the idea of having her in there, but if she can mend fences with Luca and everyone else in the clan, it will be to everyone's advantage.

If we want to have any hope for a future.

Chapter Fourteen

Robyn is as stressed as I've ever seen her, and we've been through a number of highly stressful situations at this point. I'm not sure I get it. I've dealt with Bianco, Rossi, Jimmy's antics, and I know that she's been working in the Organized Crime unit for some time.

It's unnerving to me. I have other things on my mind now.

What if the authorities decide that it's all not good enough, and that I can't sell Adria? If we learn that it's been a drug hub for years, how would we keep it under wraps, so the buyers won't panic?

I have a lot of worries that have nothing to do with Luca or whatever stupid decisions he might have made. I need to find where that fund is hidden, and I don't even know where to begin.

It's come to this—me, the boss, hiding in the bathroom. I've decided to start with Sofia. I don't know that my parents would ever share anything like that with an outsider, but she's not just any outsider. She's picked up many things over the years.

I meet her in the lobby after sneaking past Robyn.

"I just have a quick question," I tell her. "Do you remember my parents ever talking about a rainy-day fund or anything like it? The FBI is poking around, and I have no idea what they're talking about."

She regards me with caution. "Why do you think I would?"

"Because no one who's related to me by blood is telling me anything, and it's frustrating. I thought you might have heard something."

Sofia weighs her words carefully. "If your parents didn't want anyone to overhear things, chances are no one did. They were always generous and friendly, but cautious. So, if that fund exists, I can't tell you who might know. Is there a reason we're discussing this in the lobby and not in your office?"

"Yes," I admit.

"Because Agent Johnson is in your office?"

"Her focus is elsewhere," I say which is not entirely wrong. "It needs to be. I said I'd look into it."

"Okay. I'm sorry I couldn't help you, but you know I'll come to you first if I learn anything."

"Thank you."

I get back into the elevator. Two floors before mine, Luca gets in. He's looking stressed. Try living my life, cousin, I think. I've had some sympathy for him before, but he's responsible for much of this mess. It's one thing to have to deal with homophobic family. I have an idea—Lorenzo was my uncle after all. But not everyone who's had bigots in their lives becomes a drug runner. I've felt pretty vengeful at times in my life. I didn't lie to Robyn—I do like the luxury life.

But there are boundaries, for me, anyway.

"So, your business partners are still on board with having me in the meeting?"

"Yes, of course, or I'd have told you otherwise." He looks around nervously.

"No one's listening in on us," I say. "What is going on with you?"

"We can't be too careful with these people. They have a lot of influence in high places."

"I wasn't going to be careless. I understand there's a lot of money on the line."

"There is. That's why we might have come up with an idea."

This one of the rare moments I'm truly scared. This needs to be over. Is it too much to ask that people in this company listen to me?

"What would that be?"

The elevator doors open, a couple of my chief officers waiting. Luca shakes his head.

When we are in my office, I tell Robyn who's still going over papers in the sitting area, "Could you please leave us alone for a moment?" I'm not wearing the wire right now, but I'd hope that she trusts me that much at this point.

"Sure," she says, acknowledging Luca with a nod. He ignores her.

"You are pretty impolite given that she decided against pressing charges," I say when she's on the other side of the door.

"We've been over this. I didn't realize what exactly Bruno was going to do until he carried her out, all tied up."

Careful. The image he evokes makes me nauseated with anger all over again. I wish I could throw him out on his ass right here and now.

"Yeah. So, what's that about this alternative idea?"

He sends a longing look to the small, but exclusive liquor cabinet in the corner. No such luck. There's no drinking in the office at this time of day.

"We could meet at *Catania*...or here—"

"Are you fucking out of your mind?" I start speaking before he has even finished the sentence. "Do you even know what *Catania* means? Or the business we've built here? No way!"

"Relax," he says. "I was going to talk it over with you first. It's lucrative business."

"It's killing people."

"Like Al and Angela never signed off on anything like that. Or you."

"My parents are *dead*," I remind him sharply. "You will not speak about them. And no, they never got into drug trade. This is why I still had the chance to clean things up."

I might have made a mistake, I realize, when I see understanding dawn on his face.

"You told the FBI?"

"I didn't say that. I'm not suicidal. I wouldn't go with you into the meeting if your partners had any reason to doubt me. All I want is to get this over with so we can sell Adria and be done with it. The way you seem to come up with even more bizarre ideas so easily tells me the sooner the better."

"What happened to you?" he asks.

"What happened to you, Luca? You used to be decent."

"And where did that get me, really? My father hated me. No one took me seriously until I was running with the bigshots. I'm surprised you of all people don't understand. We have so little time. Why shouldn't we take what we can get?"

I'm about to argue, when I remember Robyn stating how some of my business practices weren't "victimless crimes." I still have a lot more on my side of the scale. The foundation, for example. None of the men in the family ever had much of an interest in it after Dad died. No, I can argue about my crimes, and about how many people have been helped because of them. I don't think Luca can.

"That's a philosophical question for another day. We can't rely on the previous generation anymore. We have to make our own decisions now, and if you don't want all of this to bite you, we have to stick to the plan."

To my surprise, he nods. His words are not so encouraging.

"Do you even care?"

"Our great-grandparents built this from the ground up. Yes, I do care. I'm not going to mess this up," I assure him.

"Okay then."

"Just like that? You think they're going to walk away?"

"They will," he says, slumping into the spot where Robyn sat earlier. "As long as I do that one last deal."

With Luca, there's always a caveat. I sit down next to him, more than tempted to break out the alcohol. "Tell me," I say.

So he does. Robyn knocks on the door a few minutes later, giving me an intent look.

"We're all right in here?"

Luca jumps to his feet and flees the room.

"Yes, of course," I answer her question. "We're all fine. Would you like some whiskey?"

When the day arrives, I'm calmer than I thought I would be. I know that Robyn's people have been carefully keeping tabs on Luca. They know when and how to intervene.

Regardless, it makes me a little nervous to remember Dad went into a similar situation, an event where he thought he'd be safe. On the FBI's side, capable people were in charge.

Dad never made it out of the room, regardless of the fact that Blake, Robyn's father, had worked out a deal with him.

I'm not especially scared or superstitious, but the similarities are too obvious. Before the driver takes me to Adria, Robyn and her team meet me at the office. I'm getting wired up once again. This is my property. They will not search me—or will they? I won't take any chances.

Robyn helps me zip up my dress.

"You're going to be okay," she says. Perhaps she's aware of what's on my mind.

"It can't all end here anyway. I'm not ready to have any of my cousins handle the company. If Luca's any indication, they're going to drive it into the ground."

"That's not going to happen. We're on standby, remember? As soon as you're uncomfortable, you'll let us know."

"Did you find out more about who left the photo? As much as I enjoy the hotel living, I'd like to go back to my condo at some point."

"I understand. We're working on it."

"Work harder," I say. "Not meaning you in particular. I know you work hard. It's just...unsettling."

"I know." When no one else is around for a few moments, she draws me into a brief hug. "Good luck. It will be okay. I promise." That's what Dad believed. I can't quite shake the thought.

"You better keep that promise. Remember all those grandkids I've planned for."

"I remember," she says, barely hiding the smile. "All right. Off you go. There will be agents in the main room and in the neighboring office as we've discussed. Everyone will be discreet. You go in, listen, if necessary, lay out that you've decided to sell in order to focus on the Mancini Group."

"I think I can remember that. Piece of cake. Okay. Let's do this."

That uneasy feeling stays with me regardless, my mind insisting on going through a quick slideshow of the recent horror events. That call. My mother falling sick. Bruno revealing himself to be the paranoid creepy stalker he really is, and Tony Bianco pulling the trigger on me.

I have a lot left to do. I hope I haven't used up all those second chances yet.

Robyn leans close, and I think it's because she needs to hide some wire, but instead she whispers, "I love you."

And that's just cruel, but it does snap me back into reality.

Chapter Fifteen

At Adria, it's business as usual in the restaurant and bar space. We set up in an office on the same floor as the restaurant, far enough to be unobtrusive, close enough to intervene quickly if the need arises. Two agents in the main room. We are prepared for everything. Except I wasn't prepared for the words that tumbled out of my mouth, and now I have to pay extra attention.

There is a reason why I shouldn't be here. There's a reason why I can't stay away, and you guessed it, they're the same. I'm grateful that Ryan is managing a lot of the business at the Mancini group, but now Rachel put me in charge of Kendall's safety.

I had to say it. She was drifting, maybe wondering about what could go wrong, and I brought her right back.

Kendall is cool and calm when she meets with Luca in the office space that is part of Adria.

Listening to her voice is calming me too.

"You're early," he says.

"I still own most of this company, and I'm interested in what's going on in it," Kendall returns. "Were there any more question on the other side?"

"No. They're just going to give me the details on the last deal we agreed on. Then this will be over, I swear."

"I hope you're right. The sale will go through next week."

"You never cease to remind me. I still think it's a bad idea."

I hear the whizzing of a cell phone on vibration.

"And here they are."

"You made them use the freight elevator?"

Thank you, Kendall. This is valuable information. I assume they'll leave the same way.

"They don't want to run into the other guests. I don't want them to do that either."

"I see."

I can sense the suppressed anger in her tone, and I understand why. It's fairly impossible he could keep it a secret from all employees. There are more sounds, and then the footsteps of several people.

"Showtime," I say.

Hampton's gaze is pensive. "You think she's up to this?"

I resent him for asking that question now. "I wouldn't have sent her in if I didn't think she was. I know what I'm doing."

"I wasn't saying otherwise."

The next few parts of the conversation are mostly between Luca and his guests, detailing the upcoming deal in language that pretty much sounds like code. I count three different men.

As the meeting is coming to a close, Kendall says, "My cousin here will do his part. He assured me that after that, you will terminate business with our family."

One of the men laughs. "Yeah, sure."

"Those are the last drugs?"

"Why do you care?" another one asks. "This isn't your business."

"In case Luca neglected to inform you, I'm the majority shareholder," she says coldly. "So, everything that goes down under my roof is my business."

I hope she won't overdo it.

"You said there wouldn't be any problem."

"There isn't," Luca says quickly. "She's just worried about appearances. The sale and all. Right, Kendall?"

"Or she's trying to get something on the record. Are you?"

"That's crazy. Why would I jeopardize this sale, and my business in general? I'm expecting record profits from this real estate deal. No, I have no intention of getting anything on the record. I just want you to be done with whatever it is you're doing with that heroin. That's what it is, right? Forgive my ignorance, this isn't my expertise."

"You checked her for a wire, didn't you?"

Luca hesitates just a heartbeat too long, and I curse. The plan was to give the go ahead to the agents when Luca's business partners come out of the room, but I don't think we can wait that long.

"This is ridiculous," Kendall says sharply. "Let's end this right here. And don't ever set foot on one of my properties ever again."

"Or what?"

"Now would be a really good time to end this," she says, and I know for certain that those words are for me. I signal to Rachel, and she gives the sign.

When I walk into the room, I'm dumbfounded for a few seconds. I recover instantly, but one of the men that are being led out in handcuffs is giving me an ugly grin.

"Told you we'd meet again," he says.

"Yeah, right, and you're the one going to prison. Again. This time they won't let you out."

I have to take a moment to sort out what the hell this means. Now is not that moment, for the memory of another arrest, or the considering the implications of this one. I watch as one of the other agents cuffs Kendall. She winces.

Like Ryan, most of my colleagues think she's getting off too easily.

"What the hell is this?" Luca yells. "Kendall!"

I don't care much if he knows that she played him, but one of the other men is still within earshot.

"Don't be ridiculous," I tell Luca. "We're arresting all of you. That includes her."

I wait until most of the law enforcement personnel and their charges are gone, then walk over to Kendall and remove the cuffs.

"Sorry about that," I say. "We had to make it look good."

"I know."

She looks a bit shell-shocked, for a different reason, I guess. "So that part is over."

I want to pull her close, but it's not possible. It will be a while before we can be alone.

"It is. Come on, let's go."

Chapter Sixteen

I am more than ready to leave. When I get up, the room spins for a second, something I become fully aware of when Robyn steadies me.

"Head rush," I say quickly. "I'm fine."

She nods but stays close which is more reassuring than I care to admit.

This is it. This is the end of life as I knew it, when I thought there were still people in my family I could count on—because Claudia and Elena won't feel much like joining forces once they hear that Luca was arrested. Sofia is technically not my family.

Is this what Dad tried to avoid? Or what he had in mind? I guess I'll never know.

I feel lost.

"Please tell me that I can go home and have a drink soon. I need it."

She gives me an apologetic look. Before she can answer, Hampton McKay joins us. He overheard my question.

"I'm afraid we'll have to spend some time at the office, but we'll do the major part of it starting tomorrow. I expect Mr. Mancini will want to sort out details with his lawyer too. I assume it won't be Ms. Winter?"

"No. He has his own."

"Okay, this is what we're going to do," Robyn decides. "We'll go to the field office, see what we need to go over right now. I agree, it won't be long."

"I suppose you'll stay with Ms. Mancini?"

For a heartbeat or so, both of us simply stare at him until we realize he's talking about the order Carr gave earlier. It's not a revelation. They still don't know who came to deliver the picture.

Of course, Robyn will stay.

"Yes. We can't be too careful," she says.

To my relief, Robyn and Hampton haven't promised too much. After a quick debriefing, Robyn and I can go back to the hotel while Luca is sorting out his situation with the help of his lawyers. I have told them everything I know from the beginning—regarding Luca and his deals anyway. That last deal is not going to happen now, and no one died. It's a win.

As soon as we are in the suite, I go straight to the bathroom and start running a bath. I order a bottle of champagne and some food from room service.

Robyn watches me carefully but doesn't comment.

"What?" I say anyway. "Now there's nothing we can do but wait, right?"

"I'm aware," she answers, sounding as tired as I am. "I'll wait for room service if you want to go in."

"Thank you."

So far, most of my clever plans have become unraveled. Ironically, when I've been working with Robyn, things seem to work out better. For the other side anyway—or maybe sides have changed—hell if I know. In any case, I'm glad Luca's out. And with him, the people who came to the meeting tonight.

I am about to undress when my phone vibrates on the dresser.

That was to be expected.

"What the hell is wrong with you?" Claudia yells at me. "We lose our father, now you throw Luca to the wolves?"

"I didn't do anything. He got too cozy with the wolves—if you will. Really, running drugs out of Adria? Did you know about that?"

She grows silent.

"Yes or no?" I think she's aware I have the moral higher ground for the moment, and I intend to use it. "I'm sorry about Lorenzo, but you all did this behind my father's back, and mine. I don't want anything to do with that kind of business."

Claudia laughs bitterly. "This is how you treat family. I had some sympathy after all the tragedy, and how Dad spoke about you and Luca, but you're letting everyone down."

"I'm sorry, but from where I stand, it looks like I'm holding everything together. It doesn't look like anyone else is making an effort."

"I can't believe this. I don't know you anymore, Kendall."

For some reason, that strikes a chord. I have changed in the past years, and months, so much I hardly recognize myself anymore. I'm not sure if it's a bad thing. "Luca has representation. Let's talk tomorrow."

"Right, whenever things get uncomfortable, you back away, right? Didn't your father want you to come to that fundraiser, and you couldn't find the time?"

I end the call without goodbye.

Fortunately, room service has arrived, and the delivery has been okayed by my bodyguard. She opens the door after a quick rap.

"I wasn't sure where you wanted this..."

"I'll take care of it, thanks."

I go over to the cart and pour two glasses of champagne.

"I can't," Robyn says quickly. "Technically I'm still working."

"Suit yourself." I can't argue over this now. Instead, I undress, leave my clothes on the floor where I'm standing. Her eyes widen. As tired as I am, I still notice. I pick up my glass and walk naked into the bathroom, knowing that she follows me, with her gaze anyway. "I didn't think you needed an invitation."

With a sigh, half amused half irritated, Robyn joins me in the bathroom and gets out of her clothes as well. I'm already immersed in warm water and bubbles while she's still folding both our outfits.

"You don't have to do that."

"Don't you ever feel like mundane tasks allow you to pretend you're in control of something? Despite the cryptic statement, she takes off her bra and panties. The set is an interesting choice for a day at work. Perhaps she had hopes?

"Sometimes," I admit and make room so she can sit and lean back against me. I brush my hand over her shoulder. With every official action, our first moments together seem far and unreal...I want to go back there. I want more. But there are other things we need to take care of first.

"How do you think it went?"

"As expected."

"But?" That tiny bit of hesitation didn't go unnoticed with me. "There's something you aren't telling me."

She chuckles. "There are things you aren't telling me. You did a great job. You don't need to know everything."

"Not even when I need to feel in control of something?"

"All right, I don't see the harm. One of the men we arrested tonight...He's bad news."

"No kidding. Aren't they all?"

"Not like that."

Her tone makes me sober up quickly. "Is there something I *should* know?"

"It's complicated. We need to focus on wrapping this up. Tomorrow." She takes my hand, running it over her body, a clear indication that this conversation is over. I'm going to need reassurances.

"We're going to come back to this?"

"I don't think we'll have a choice. It will be part of the wrapping up. But not now."

"You want some of that champagne now?" I ask softly, touching my lips against her neck. I don't need any more prompting to touch her.

"No. I want you."

We leave the tub, and towel off as quickly as humanly possible, still dripping and shivering when we make it to the bed. In a matter of heartbeats, body heat changes the temperature quickly. Robyn is on top of me, no longer hesitant as she kisses me deeply, her hand brushing over my hip and sliding between my thighs. I can't hold back the blissful gasp, all the stress and worries of the past days slipping away.

Finally, this plan worked.

Chapter Seventeen

I am so grateful that Kendall is on the same page. Tomorrow is going to be difficult, and we both must stay in our designated lanes. For now, we don't have a care in the world, desire the only focus.

It's also a relief to no longer pretend. It might be complicated, impossible, but we've tried to keep our hands off of each other. It doesn't work. It will never work. We might as well accept the inevitable.

Kendall kisses her way down my body in an unhurried way, making me squirm and moan, feeding the fire. When she finally leans in for a taste, I'm trembling with anticipation, and it's everything she promised. We can forget about who we are. It doesn't matter—or maybe it's the opposite, I don't know anymore.

I've been looking over my shoulder for a long time, occupational hazard, necessity, I've been doing it on the job and in private. My initial assignment with her required it.

For the first time in a long time, I feel safe, even if it's irrational.

"I love you too," she whispers.

ell

Kendall has her secrets. I have mine. For the time being, it might be better to keep it that way, even though I sense that she's suspecting something. I talk to Hampton and Rachel via videocall on my tablet, and to my surprise, they both tell me not to come in at the moment.

"Why not?" I ask. Kendall is in the bathroom, so I feel safe showing my irritation.

"It's an order. From your supervisor," Rachel reminds me, only a faint trace of sarcasm in her voice.

"Is there any particular reason for this order? Like last night's arrest?"

Now, her irritation mirrors mine. "Robyn, we're pretty busy here. If I remember correctly, you also have a job to do, stick close to Ms. Mancini and make sure no one erases her out of the picture."

"I could do some work from the office."

"We have someone on that picture. You are in that hotel room for a reason. I don't have time to argue with you."

"So, this has nothing to do with the fact that Brad Dolan was part of that gang?"

"We'll deal with Dolan, and Mr. Mancini. Don't worry about it."

Now I do worry about it. Since the beginning of this case, I've taken so many actions that were not part of the initial plan. Kendall returns to the main room, giving me a pensive look.

"Well, so far things have been quiet, except Kendall's cousin called. She's not happy."

Rachel sighs. "I expected that. But with them busy, and the members of the Bianco family that haven't been arrested hunkering down with their lawyers as well, things *are* fairly quiet. That's good news."

I assume she's right.

Kendall waves to the screen. "SAC Carr, good morning. Any ETA when I can return to my condo? As you know I have a big sale coming up."

"Yes, about that. It will be necessary for you to postpone. At the moment, we'd like you to stay where you are with Agent Johnson."

To my surprise, Kendall shrugs. "No problem. I'll call the buyers to reschedule."

"Thank you for your cooperation."

"What can I say? Confined to a five-star hotel room with Agent Johnson, it's a hardship, but I'll survive."

Rachel isn't the most humorous person I know, but she laughs. "I can see you'll be okay. Robyn, I have to go. Hampton, Ryan, or I will be in touch."

"Okay. Thank you. Talk to you later."

I end the call, aware of Kendall's gaze on me. She doesn't say anything, and I'm starting to find it a bit unnerving. "What?"

"Brad Dolan, who is he?"

"Someone I busted once, but I guess you figured that out already. It's not important."

Kendall perches on the edge of an armchair.

"It's obviously important to you, or you wouldn't feel the need to be there."

"How much of that call did you spy on?"

"I won't pretend I'm not freaked out about these latest developments. Frankly, when you all suggested I should get wired to talk to my cousin, I thought it was extreme. Yesterday was extreme. Up until then, I could maybe pretend that Luca was just scared of his father, that he understood that covering for Jimmy was horribly wrong...Yet, here we are. I'm not sure what's going to happen tomorrow, to the business, my life...us. And it is freaking me out. Your turn."

"What do you mean?" There's only so long I can stall—but I will try. "No, not what you're thinking right now. Not the worst-case scenario, but it got close. Bad hostage situation. I got caught in the middle."

I realize I revealed a lot more than I intended to when I see her face go pale.

"I am so sorry."

"For what? You did what we asked of you. I understand that at the cabin, you were trying to take care of me first. And later, when you were asked to wear the wire, you didn't protest...much."

"True." I can tell from her rueful tone that I've been spot-on.

"Honestly, the money you've been shifting away from the government over time, it's something that needs correcting, but hell, I've seen worse. A lot worse."

"I've asked myself a lot of questions lately. I've been around men like that, pretty much all my life. I'm wondering if there's ever a situation where the end justifies the means. I'm wondering about some of the things my father ordered done."

I'm not sure if I can help her with this.

"I want to do better," she says. "Our foundation does good work. We have always tried to look out for people more vulnerable than us. I realize that might not be enough."

"You'll be fine."

Rachel is right—being in these surroundings, I shouldn't complain. In fact, I should be glad to have others deal with Dolan.

"We will be," Kendall corrects me. "I know we're stuck together for the time being. I'm not going to hound you, but if you want to talk, I can listen."

What a strange offer coming from her. Then again...We have come to this point. Where there is an "us." Perhaps it's not the worst thing.

"Thank you, I appreciate it. But now I think we need coffee. It was a short night."

The distraction works. Kendall smiles. "It was. To be honest, I see a series of short nights in our future, so I better call that room service."

I smile back at her and go to the bathroom where I open the faucet, staring at my mirror image for a few tense, stubborn moments before the tears fall and I look away. I don't even realize I forgot to lock the door until Kendall is in the room with me, holding me close. I'm beyond embarrassed, but all of a sudden, I can't stop crying.

"I know you said the worst-case scenario didn't happen, but I know you a little by now," she says calmly. "I might not have as much power as before, but I still know people who owe me favors, and they get the job done. Just let me know what you need."

The temptation has never been this great—since that day.

—ele—

Kendall is on the phone for most of the morning, and she doesn't seem to mind me eavesdropping—not that she has the right to say no under the current conditions. The buyers, her lawyers, the chief officers...I'm starting to drift which is not a good thing. I lied to her. It was the worst-case scenario.

And perhaps that's the reason why I didn't resist much, threw myself head over heals into this ill-fated affair.

Because the last time I hesitated, I didn't get a second chance. Or any chance at all.

I shouldn't complain about being in close quarters with a beautiful woman, but it's driving me nuts that I can't do anything, figure out who broke into her apartment, or interrogate Dolan. Not that Rachel would let me near him again, given the history we have. I could take Kendall up on her offer, but then I'd have to tell her the truth. I'm not ready. Not because I'm afraid of judgment. Kendall Mancini has little room to judge, and she's not that kind of person anyway...but because I would have to feel the truth behind those words we exchanged. Like I said, I'm not ready.

Chapter Eighteen

It's a busy morning for me, not so much for Robyn who has little to do other that watch me make calls. I'm not much the wiser, on anything, a few hours later.

Everyone I talk to is polite. The longer this goes on, the less likely prison is for me, but there are precautions I need to take. Especially now when it's not just about me.

Especially now when the matter is more urgent.

"You're not going to like this," I start.

"But it will all be for the greater good?" she suggests wryly.

"Eventually, I promise. First, it will be for my good, and potentially yours. I have to go to my office."

"Absolutely not. We still have no clue who left that picture behind, and what they're planning next. It might have been a warning."

"I get that. Regardless, I have to show my face. There's too much going on, and people have to see that I'm still running this business. Come on, this is what I have a bodyguard for. And you've guarded my body in the best possible ways."

"Kendall. Give it a few days. We have no leads. It's too dangerous."

"If you think they're this clever, don't you think they know we're here? If we moved around, we wouldn't be sitting ducks?"

She winces at that.

"We're not sitting ducks. A team would be here within minutes if I need it."

"Really?" For a moment, I'm a bit taken aback by that. "I'm this important to you guys? Wow. That aside, it's really important that I go. Check in with your boss, tell her that, if necessary, I pay for people's extra shifts."

That makes her laugh, and perhaps that was my only intention.

"You know it doesn't work that way, but I'll ask her."

"Thank you. I swear I'm taking this as seriously as I need to. I don't want you or anyone to get hurt. Hell, I don't want to get hurt again."

"All right. I'll just let them know."

"Be careful and don't stay longer than you have to," I hear SAC Carr advise. Robyn's lips tighten in a thin line. She was hoping Carr would say no.

Lucky for me, she doesn't.

I need to do this, and I need to do it soon before the situation deteriorates. It's hard to say how serious the person who broke into the condo was. One the one hand, they could have surprised us in our sleep. On the other hand, as Robyn said, this might only have been the first warning.

"In and out. I promise."

"Sure. Let's get this over with."

Robyn is tense as we walk down the hall to the elevator, and to my parked car in the garage. Out on the street, an unmarked car follows us—one of Carr's conditions. I hope they won't all come up with us, but I can't really tell her why either. Not yet. It's not ideal right now, but once all is said and done, it will be the best for both of us. Temporary maybe, but best.

If all goes well...Okay, that's a big if at the moment. I can't wait to see her face if this surprise works out. Given whatever her history with Dolan and others is I know one thing for sure. We've both earned a break from petty little men, and a few days of mandatory isolation in a nice hotel won't do it. We've both given a lot.

On the fifth floor, a couple tries to get in, all but shrinking back from Robyn's hard stare and unmistakable gesture.

"Was that really necessary?"

"Is it really necessary for you to go to the office?"

I keep my mouth shut until we arrive. She'll understand. Soon enough.

—ele

The problem is that while I'm in the office, she is too. How am I going to play this? She is not to leave my side.

It's too early to come full circle. It's not that I don't trust her, but...

In the midst of my musings, the phone rings, and I stall by picking up. Robyn stands in the corner. She hasn't lost the tense look.

To my surprise, it's Elena.

"Hey. How are you doing?"

"How do you think I'm doing?" she asks. "My husband has a boyfriend. He's about to go to prison. Thank you so much, Kendall, you're doing a splendid job taking care of all of us."

I'm stunned. I'd expected her to be unhappy with the situation, understandably though...but it was Lorenzo and Luca who usually boasted about taking care of family. I had no idea my duties extended this far—and they've all lived a cushy life from the profits of the Mancini Group and Adria. I was going to pay them their share. For sure, it's not my fault that Luca is gay—or that he made deals with a man who was implicated in "bad hostage situations."

"I'm sorry you feel that way. Luca was associating with dangerous people. They put all of us and the business at risk."

"Like your father never did. Or you."

"I'm not going to discuss this with you any longer."

"That's the problem, isn't it? You've been deciding everything, for everybody, by yourself."

"I'm hanging up now."

"Sure, you do that. You'll be fine, with the FBI protecting you."

Okay, maybe I can't end the call right away. "Wait a minute, what does that mean? You know that this is all about damage control. We give a little, we don't all end up under a bridge?"

"You gave them my husband," she says bitterly.

"Your husband stood by while a woman was beaten up. So, it was about time," I snap and finally click the end call button.

"Trouble?" Robyn's voice is calm. I take a deep breath.

"Not as long as we keep our distance for a while."

"Now what are we really here for?"

"To make sure I'm up to date with what's going on in my company. Just a few more minutes." I settle behind my desk, thinking about writing a quick email. I reconsider and head for the bathroom. Robyn takes one, two steps before I say, "Sorry, we're not at that stage in our relationship yet. I'm warning you. Probably never."

With a wry grin, she steps back.

I lock the door of the bathroom, and after a few moments, flush and open the faucet. After washing my hands, I leave the water running, just like Robyn did the previous night when she didn't want me to hear her cry. Then I call Sofia. I have to think of better ways in the future. I can't leave too many traces.

"Hey."

"Hey," she says dryly. "You've made quite the splash."

"I need to ask you another favor. Could you please come to the office quick, come up and distract my shadow for a few minutes? I'll have coffee delivered—"

"You don't need to bribe me with coffee, but what are you up to?"

"I promise this will all make sense eventually."

She is silent. "Some people in your family are pretty angry at you."

"I'm aware. I'm pretty angry at Luca for doing dirty business out of Adria, but here we are. Please?"

"Okay, sure, but only because I'm curious to know what this is all about."

"Great. I just need you to talk to her a bit, so she won't be watching me all the time. See you in a bit."

"Yes, you will." She sounds amused, but I know I can rely on her. Relieved, I return to the office where Robyn waits for me, regarding me with a gaze that's too suspicious for my liking.

"I swear, I'm not trying to prolong this unnecessarily. The sooner we can go back, the sooner we can think of...other things."

"Sounds like a plan. So, what do we do now?"

"More calls," I say, and for those, I don't have to hide in the bathroom.

Ten minutes later, there's a knock on the door. Robyn goes to check, and she lets Sofia in. Game on. Now I have to be quick.

"Hi, Kendall, it's so good to see you." Sofia hugs me quickly and shakes Robyn's hand. "Agent Johnson."

"Sofia, hey." I give her a prompting look. Bless her, she came up with a cover story on the way here.

"I came to do some work, but since you're here, I wanted to let you know I can shift things on my desk around a bit, help wherever it's needed."

"That's a great idea." I cast a quick look at Robyn who is still listening. I can tell her attention isn't focused on the content of the conversation, but on the surroundings, which is a good thing. "I can fill you in, but how about I get us some coffee and snacks? Robyn, it's going to be an hour at the most, but I have hope it could be faster. Sofia here is very savvy."

"Go ahead," Robyn says. "As long we're here now...I'm going to check them before they come in."

"I've had the same chef for almost a decade. If they want to poison me now..." I abandon the sentence. It's not the time to make jokes. The office can only be accessed from one door. I make the call to the kitchen, then give the phone to Robyn. My employees are fairly used to having her and her people around. A lot of effort for a cup of coffee and pastry, but it will all be worth it in the end.

The moment Robyn has left the room I head over to the painting on the far wall. It's an original. Dad gave it to me when I first had an office in the company. When I moved into his, I brought it with me.

Mind you, this painting alone is worth quite a bit. I take it off the wall and turn it around.

Sofia, leaning against the door, regards me with an amused look.

"I can never figure you out, Kendall. I thought you two were on the same page."

"We are. We will be. And I won't forget about you either." I'm looking at the back of the painting, running my fingers along the frame.

"Is this some sort of riddle? Your dad loved them."

No kidding. Something he said when he gave me that painting sprang to mind the other day.

Just remember, your future will always be secure.

Nothing about a college fund.

But there's a sequence of numbers written on the back, in the corner, so tiny that I have to squint. I write it down, put the paper in my pocket and hang the painting just the moment Robyn comes back in. An approved employee from the kitchen brings coffee and fresh raspberry muffins.

I feel a lot better. I know what to do now.

I can't do it here, not all of it, because at some point the lure of coffee and baked goods, and Sofia's conversational skills, will not be enough to distract Robyn. That, and I don't want those interactions to be traced.

I spend a little longer going over the daily work and make a few quick calls before I declare the workday over. It's not even noon yet.

"Okay, I think we're done here for the moment. Sofia, thank you again for coming. I'll email you the rest. Robyn?"

"Sure. Let's go home."

Chapter Nineteen

K endall is up to something, and I'm going to find out what it is. I didn't believe the whole set-up for a minute. She might have forgotten about the access I had from the early days of our relationship. The surveillance.

Imagine my surprise when she went straight for the painting.

"What are you doing?" she asks when we are back at the hotel, and I quickly turn off my phone.

"Just checking in with my team. No news on the intruder."

"Dolan?" she asks, and I'm stunned to realize I almost forgot about him. No longer my problem.

"Nothing yet, but I don't see a problem. We have a recording."

"Okay. Then I guess my irate relatives are all I have to deal with. You won't believe this...There was a time when I thought about involving Claudia and Elena more. I guess that's not going to happen. They'll still get their checks though as long as I can hold on to the Group...and apparently, I'll have to hold on to Adria a bit longer."

She sounds wistful. I suppress the urge to apologize. This isn't my fault. She's not completely innocent either, but the situation is unfortunate. All around. I wanted to do some research on my own before I confronted her with this. I'm frustrated with myself because I feel like I owe her, and with Kendall, because she's still acting like she has room for error at this point.

"What the hell?" I blurt out.

"What's wrong?"

Perhaps I can't blame her for her confusion. That did come out of nowhere.

"You know what I mean. Your little diversion. You know we shouldn't even be outside this room at the moment. So, what was so important that you were willing to risk your life and mine, oh, and Sofia's?" She's not the real recipient of all that anger, but she's the only one I can direct it at now. I'm still mad at Rachel for not involving me where I could possibly help more—and Dolan, but that's another story. I have reason to be mad at Kendall as well. Perhaps I expected too much of her. To tell me the truth. "Make no mistake, you're going to tell me what this was all about. Because right now we have a deal, and it's a little precarious. We've gone out of our way to accommodate you, and your business—"

"I didn't leave you empty-handed," she reminds me.

"Now's not the time. If you're doing something stupid, I don't know that I can keep you out of prison."

It's a tell that my voice sounds slightly panicky, and she hasn't missed it.

"Robyn. Relax. Winter and Dunne have it under control, and besides, like you said, you already cut me a lot of slack. Revoking all of that would not make anyone look good, and it might jeopardize the convictions you already have. Carr doesn't want that."

"Did you hear a single word I said?" I'm frustrated.

"I heard everything, from the moment we met. All right."

"No bullshit?"

She gives me a wry smile. "I would have liked for us to have this conversation later, but I give you my word. This is the truth. Remember when I asked you if you were ready to leave your job behind?"

"That was never a question, and you know it. What did you do?"

"Sit down, please."

"Why?"

She produces a phone I've never seen before, and I groan. A burner phone.

"You were pretty outraged over your cousin's dealings at Adria. Are you sure you're not a tiny bit hypocritical?"

"Ouch. That depends. This is not something created from drug money. It's a secret getaway, and if necessary, a last resort."

"For whom?" I don't understand anything at the moment.

"The infamous college fund. I think we both thought it would be about money stashed away somewhere, and maybe it still is, I don't know. But this is a phone number."

"On the back of the painting?"

"You saw that, huh? Is that surveillance still legal?" she returns.

"Come on."

"Legit question. Anyway, yes. My dad gave that painting to me when I got an office in the company. A long time ago."

This is interesting indeed. "What does it mean?"

"It means if I ever need a way out, I'll call that number. And I think they'd be okay with me bringing a plus one."

I don't know what to say. This is beyond some bizarre fantasy, and I still have to deal with the stalker, Dolan, and the bigger picture of this case.

"Why would you need it? You've always been visible. You seem to like it, and you told me over and over again that you're willing to cut ties with the less...legal parts of your business."

"I didn't lie to you," she says calmly. "I'm also not crazy. If that stalker, or whatever we want to call him, becomes a bigger problem—or if the prosecutors change their minds, I won't sit around waiting." Her tone becomes teasing when she ads, "You wouldn't miss me a little bit?"

"Oh, don't worry. I don't know what to do without you anymore."

"I'm a bit hurt by the sarcasm, but I guess I earned it. This is the last secret. I promise. I didn't even realize until today where I needed to look. Dad could be quite subtle with these things."

"Did you call the number?"

"No, I think it's meant for emergencies. But you say the word, and we're off. I'm serious, Robyn. I'm not going to leave you behind."

It's odd, the way her words send a shiver skittering down my spine. I'm not sure how long I can keep the memories at bay. It was a given that I'd be confronted with them someday, after everything I've done. Part of me wants to believe her. And another part knows that there will always be surprises with Kendall Mancini. Take it or leave it. But what does that mean for my career, my life?

"Thank you," I say, and that, at least, sounds honest. "I don't think we're there yet. We will find who broke into your condo, and who paid him. You'll clean up the business, and there will be no reason for you to hide."

"What if I still chose to? Would you come with me?"

"I don't know." While we're being honest. "I guess putting my life in someone's hands like that would be terrifying." Because I did it before, and see what happened.

"I get that. Well, let's see how this plays out. I guess I don't have to involve Sofia any longer, since you know now...I can trust you, right?"

"I won't tell anyone." This time, there's no hesitation. I've already broken too many rules.

That night, I accept a glass of champagne even though I know I shouldn't, and I try to keep all those self-loathing thoughts at bay when we're in bed together. Intimacy is easy, uncomplicated, surprisingly unburdened by the facts of our lives.

For a few unreal moments, I allow myself the vision of what life would be like, with her, hidden away somewhere. It's quite beautiful in my mind. I know it can't last. Even when I hold her close to me, listening to her rapid heartbeat, once more realizing that I'm in over my head...I couldn't, I wouldn't ever go this far—would I?

There's a small voice asking why not? All my career I've come across people who just take, no matter who gets hurt. I don't put Kendall into this category. At least she's tried to steer the ship into a different direction. The stories about her father vary depending on who tells them, but I tend to believe that Sofia Bianco's is a significant one.

I used to think we could make a difference, make the world a better place for a fairer, thriving society. At the very least, take out enough trash at a time so we wouldn't get overwhelmed. I am overwhelmed right now, and feeling guilty, because the idea of her whisking me away from all this sounds so good.

"Are you okay?" she asks softly, predictably, because I'm crying. That's even worse. I don't like to be vulnerable. Weak, the little inner voice scolds. I take a deep breath, trying to keep my voice steady.

"I don't think so. This hasn't been the career-boosting moment I thought it would be."

She laughs, tracing a gentle hand down my back. "I'm sorry I didn't have much to offer you except sex."

I turn to her. "Oh, you offered me a whole lot more, but I can't complain about the sex."

"Good," Kendall whispers, fingertips teasing over my nipples, turning them into hard peaks. "I wasn't done yet."

I guess I can indulge in the fantasy a little while longer.

———

In the morning I talk to Hampton who assures me that neither Dolan nor Luca Mancini will be a problem in the future.

"One of them is going to turn," he says. "Don't worry, it's not Dolan. No deals for him."

I can't hold back the relieved sigh. "Thank every deity in the universe."

"He's done, Robyn."

"Good. What about Mancini?"

"Keeping his lawyers busy. I don't expect him to get much out of it either. His involvement was pretty obvious."

I enjoy being confined with Kendall in many ways, but it still drives me crazy that I'm not doing the work, interrogations, and following up.

"Things are going as planned," I say. "He won't be trying to set up Kendall?"

"With what? She gave us everything."

Not everything, I think.

"So, she'll be okay?"

"You're serious?" he asks wryly. "Her lawyers are busy too. They keep in touch and demand regular updates. I guess you can say that yes, she'll be fine. What about you? Still enjoying the high life?"

"Come on, that was low. It's not like we're here for a vacation."

"I didn't mean to say that. Keep being careful. We might have a lead."

"Way to bury it, too. What lead? Why didn't you start with that?"

"It's not for certain yet. It is however no secret that Claudia Mancini has been angry with Kendall for some time. After Lorenzo's death, things didn't go at all like she and her brother had planned."

Kendall returns from the bathroom that moment.

"What else?" I try to keep it vague.

"She, too, had been shuffling money around, shortly before we busted him."

I watch Kendall go over to the closet and choose her outfit.

"She knew?" I ask, incredulous.

"We're not sure yet, but nothing with this family is ever coincidence. Be careful."

"I always am. Let me know if you learn anything new."

I end the call and toss the phone onto the bed. If Claudia was the culprit all along, how far do her connections go?

"We need to talk," I say.

Chapter Twenty

"**N**o way. You must be mistaken."

Robyn isn't insulted, just pensive. Somehow that is worse. Yes, I was mad at Claudia, and Luca, for that matter. He's her brother, the family has always been close, and they just lost their father.

This is a bridge too far.

"I know the people I work with," she says. "Hampton, Ryan, Rachel—they don't make statements like this on a hunch. They must have something on her."

"No. I don't believe it."

"Why?" she asks, genuinely curious. "Because she's a woman? Bianco's wife covered for him. Elena knew some things. And—"

I hold up a hand to stop her. I don't want to think about the fact that my mother was involved with some of the darker elements of the business—I know she was, because I ran it with her, and then on my own. No one is innocent.

I still don't believe that Claudia wants me dead. It has to stop somewhere.

"I don't believe it. We basically grew up together. Luca and Lorenzo bought into that macho bullshit, and they did things behind my back. I don't think she was in on it. I think someone wants her to be their scapegoat."

"And who would that be?" I don't like her calm, sympathetic tone. It makes me nervous.

"We're watching the Biancos," she says. Figure of speech—right now the only person she's watching is me.

"Bruno—people dropped him like a hot potato. He doesn't have that kind of contacts," Robyn reminds me.

"It can't be Claudia."

"If it's not her, we're running out of potential suspects. How many people have you and your family pissed off?"

I make a dismissive gesture. "You've been doing this job for how long? You know as well as I do that the people at the top don't play around. There's a message in here. If some of the other families wanted me dead, I would be. They've mostly been waiting to see what would happen between our family and the Biancos. Given that most of them are in jail right now, I guess you could say we won."

"But so is Luca. Could someone be seeing a vacuum to fill?"

Her phone rings. I have to think fast.

"I'll just go get some ice," I tell her and leave the room, hearing her response, "I have to call you back, *damn it, Kendall!*"

I am lucky to get the elevator right away. Each second seems too long. Perhaps I was naïve to think we could take what's left of the business in the right direction, together. Me, Claudia, Sofia, maybe Elena. But I can't have the rest of my family break apart like this.

I need to make it right.

I manage to get to the garage, my car and out onto the street—by now, I think Robyn is trying to get a BOLO out on me. I have to do this quick. I don't call Claudia, certain that she might not pick up. She has her own office at Adria.

I shake my head to myself with a sigh. At this point, I might just give up and call the number Dad left me.

Robyn might not think it's a good idea, but I saw the longing in her eyes. She, too, is overdue for a break, and perhaps we could start over, somewhere, together.

Maybe being cooped up in a hotel room has made me illogical. In that case, there would be no need to make up with someone who has potentially commissioned a hit on me? No.

No.

I stop the car in the parking lot and all but jog the way to the entrance. The receptionist's eyes widen when she sees me.

"Ms. Mancini. We didn't except to see you today."

"Is Claudia in?" I won't waste time trying to interpret her words.

"Yes, but I don't know if—"

"Thank you, I'll take it from here." Another elevator, too slow. There's security on the top floor, one of them getting cheeky.

"Ma'am, could you please wait here?"

"No, I couldn't. I don't have time for this, Mr...?" With a frown, he steps aside, and a moment later, I'm knocking on the door of Claudia's office. Through the frosted door, I can see her get up and come to open it. She doesn't look happy to see me, but I expected that.

"I don't have time," she snaps. "And just in case this wasn't clear enough, I don't want to see you either."

I could swear the security guard from earlier is snickering. I am not afraid. I'm just starting to get irritated.

"I know you're mad at me, but we still need to get things done here."

Claudia steps back to let me in.

"Funny, I thought you were happy hiding out with the FBI agent. Hell, everyone knows you're sleeping with her."

I don't think I should answer that.

"Someone hired a stalker—potential hitman. We had reason to take precautions."

"What does that have to do with me? My father is dead, and my brother is in prison. I'm just trying to hold things together."

"I know how that feels."

"To be betrayed by your own family?" she asks in a scathing tone. "No, Kendall, you don't know how that feels."

"Believe it or not, but I've been trying to hold things together for the past couple of years. I never meant anyone harm. The Biancos killed your father, and Luca...He brought this on himself."

"You, spying on him? I'm so tired of your excuses. Go home."

"That's the problem, I can't go home. The FBI has some ideas about who might be behind this. I told them there's no chance."

Claudia shoots me an exasperated look. "This is why you're here? To ask me if I hired someone to kill you?"

I'm not sure what to say to that, so I shrug.

"You're delusional," she accuses.

"Slow down, please. I think you've used up your share of insults. I know you don't approve of what I did, but can we talk about this like adults?"

She walks behind her desk and slumps into the chair. For several seconds, we're both silent. I'm alarmed when she leans forward and starts to cry. The end of the line? A confession?

"I'm sorry for what I did," I say. "I had no choice. This, Luca, running drugs out of Adria, it was always going to blow up. Now he has a chance to give them the other players."

"To be a rat," Claudia scoffs.

Like you. She doesn't say it, but I can read it in her expression. The unspoken reproach feels like a blow.

"To make things right." I try anyway. I find a box of tissues and hand it to her.

"Thanks," she mumbles. "Whatever they're telling you, I don't want you dead. I hate to admit it, but you have a point. We have to figure out how to continue from here."

"I know." I take a seat across from her. "But why would they think it's you? Do you have any idea who might want to set you up?"

"None whatsoever. The past few days I've been busy making sure Luca has what he needs, and I do my share of the job. I know that you must be going mad in that hotel room."

"Yes and no," I say vaguely, inappropriately reminded of some of the activities Robyn and I used to pass the time. "It's been tough. But if you find out anything, I need to know. The sooner we can put this to bed, and I can be back at work full-time, the better." Unless Robyn and I disappear into the sunset, which I've made a lot less likely with my stunt. I don't regret it. I had to do it—and I believe my cousin. "I want to visit Luca. They must allow me to do that."

"I'm sure he'd be glad to see you," Claudia says.

I search for traces of sarcasm but can't find any.

"Really?"

"Yes, really. It's tough on him too."

While I still ponder the best response, the door opens and Robyn walks in.

"Meeting's over," she says, her tone leaving no room for negotiation. Yes, it's a difficult situation. I still can't ignore how hot it is when she's trying to boss me around.

"Ms. Mancini, come with me."

Claudia's eyes are still rimmed with red while she observes the scene with a somewhat smug grin.

"I guess you have to go, Ms. Mancini. I'll see you next time."

I roll my eyes at her and get to my feet. I'll face the music with Robyn, but I feel so much better now. Not everything is crumbling around me.

I follow her back into the parking garage where we take my car. I know better then to argue when she holds up her hand.

Sitting behind the wheel, Robyn stares straight ahead, her shoulders tense with anger. I could think of ways to melt that tension away...When she looks at me, all thoughts of sensual distraction are gone in a heartbeat.

"Do you have a death wish?" she asks.

"This couldn't wait. I saved you time—Claudia certainly isn't the one. Besides, we could both use her as an ally in the future. I'm not stupid."

"I'm not going to argue with you. We'll go to the office. I'll ask someone else to be assigned to you."

"What? No. This is working. Claudia will help us!"

"What if she was pretending? You walked right into her office after I told you my colleagues had something on her. The killer could have been watching you, whether or not she's the one who put out the hit."

She's raising her voice, and we haven't even left the parking lot yet. Behind the anger, I can detect something else.

"I'm so sorry," I say. "I didn't mean to make you worry. I know what I'm doing."

She shakes her head, so I lean in and kiss her. Robyn kisses me back, with surprising passion given how tired she sounded a second ago. She fastens her hand at the back of my neck to pull me closer, pulling my hair slightly. I don't care. I almost expect us to go even further right here in the parking lot, but of course we both have jobs to do, never mind a potential killer on the loose.

"Maybe I'm the one who doesn't know. Either way, this isn't good. Hampton or Ryan can protect you better."

"No."

"No?" she repeats with a laugh as we put on our seat-belts, and she pulls out of the parking lot. "It's not up to you."

"But it's only you that I trust. You've saved my life before. That's all I need to know."

"Let's get to the office. I need to talk to some people, and I need to know that you'll stay put for a while."

"I can do that."

"I'm so glad you agree."

We don't talk for the rest of the drive.

Chapter Twenty-One

M y plan was to leave Kendall in one of the inter-
rogation rooms, provide her with a coffee and a
snack while I talk to my colleagues. I'm not sure she still
deserves a snack, but oh well, I try not to be petty.

We have barely entered the office when Rachel Carr
comes heading in our direction.

"You got my message? Good. We'll need to talk to you
later, Ms. Mancini."

"Your message about...?"

Hampton appears behind us. "Ms. Mancini, if you
could come with me? We have to talk to Agent Johnson.
This won't take long."

Kendall sends me a questioning, somewhat alarmed
look. I can only shrug. I have no idea what they are
talking about. My priority was to bring her back safe.

What do they know?

We go straight to Rachel's office where she tells me
the news.

"Judge Lawrence recused herself from the Mancini
case this morning."

"What? Why?" What I know of her work is impeccable. She's a no-nonsense person, tough but fair. She

must have good reasons. A new judge means upheaval. I'm not sure how much more I can take. I might take Kendall up on her offer to disappear and start over.

"We don't know that much yet, but what we do know is that Judge Collins will take over."

"That's not a bad thing, I assume. He has a strong anti-corruption record." Even as I say it, possible scenarios come to mind, not all of them good. "We're going to continue as planned? Keep Kendall out of prison?"

"That's the plan," Carr says. I don't like the brief hesitation on her part.

"What does that mean? She gave us Bruno, most of the Bianco family, and her own cousin. She wore a wire for the meeting with Dolan, and she saved my life."

"I know all that, and we've taken it into consideration. But remember that our cooperation with her will come to an end as we're closing cases. We don't know yet if Collins wants to look at the deal, but just in case he does…You should be prepared."

"Wow." I wipe a hand across my face, trying hard not to feel defeated at complications popping up at every turn. "It doesn't have to come to this, right? If I read Collins correctly, he wants to fry bigger fish. There's even talk about a run for governor."

"I just wanted to bring you up to date on the developments. I suppose you had something for me as well?"

"Kendall insists that Claudia can't be the one who put out the hit. I'm not yet sure about what to think, but what exactly do we have on her?"

Rachel looks at me as if I said something irrational.

"This family has had a lot of losses. Now that Luca Mancini is in prison, there's only her and Kendall left. But that's just a theory. Look at this." She produces a tablet, swiping through a number of files before she hands it to me.

There, at *Catania*, the Mancini's family restaurant, is Claudia, having dinner with a man named Arturo Rossi. He has a lot of history with both the Mancinis and the Biancos, and he's done whatever he could to put himself in a favorable position with the latter. This doesn't make sense.

"Are you sure that's what it means? She might be pursuing her own agenda, but the Mancinis aren't exactly friends with Arturo."

"We have a recording. She and Rossi are about to sign a deal to build and restore restaurants, and she said, I quote, 'Kendall doesn't need to be a part of this.'"

"They don't exactly see eye to eye on many things. I imagine Kendall wouldn't be happy. She wanted to get rid of the restaurants except for *Catania*."

"His answer is 'I'll take care of it.' Claudia: 'No worries, I already have someone on it.'"

As mad as I was at Kendall for sneaking out on me earlier, I'm sad for her now. She was so hopeful.

"That doesn't sound good. Is it enough yet to bring them in?"

"We're working on it. I don't want to rattle them and have to let them go. I'd prefer we keep Ms. Mancini in protective custody for the time being."

I nod. Now's not the time to make big changes. My other plans will have to wait.

"What about Dolan?" I have to ask.

She sighs. "Trying to pull his usual bullshit, has a fancy lawyer, but none of it will help him."

That, at least, sounds reassuring.

"Did he mention me?"

"Once or twice. You know him. There's a reason I want you far away from this."

"I'm suffering from cabin fever a bit," I admit. "I feel like I should do more."

"You're keeping our key witness alive. That is your job...Is there anything else I should know?" she asks.

"No. I'll talk to Kendall about Claudia and Rossi." And the fact that she should notify her lawyers yesterday, but I don't say that out loud. Maybe Hampton already made that recommendation. There is no way Collins can throw out the deal just like that, is there?

But just in case...I'm glad I didn't mention the rainy-day fund to anyone. One way or another this has to stop.

—ele—

Hampton has brought Kendall to the break room where they both have coffees in front of them. The scene looks a bit too amiable given the circumstances. Maybe I'm paranoid—or jealous. It's hard to tell.

"Can you leave us alone for a bit?" I ask. I swear they were both about to get to their feet. Hampton picks up his coffee before he leaves, patting my shoulder on the way out. I sit next to Kendall.

"It's not going to get easier, is it?" she asks.

I can't argue with her. I wish I could.

"Judge Lawrence recused herself today."

"So I've heard. You probably know more than me, but I can read some things between the lines. Will I be able to go back to the hotel, or should I call my lawyers now?"

"You are not under arrest."

"Yet."

"You're not under arrest," I repeat before I get up and get myself a coffee too. After I moment of consideration, I buy a small bag of chips from the vending machine. It's that kind of day.

"Come on," Kendall protests. "You can get homemade ones from the hotel."

"Yeah, well, I need them now. Things won't be moving that far, but they are in motion. So yes, I think it's a good idea to talk to your lawyers, just in case."

She regards me with curiosity.

"It's in our interest too, to keep moving. Kendall..."

As if she knows I'm about to deliver more bad news, she stalls me by stealing a few chips from my bag.

"These aren't as bad as I thought they'd be."

"You're such a snob." I can't help it, and I'm glad to hear her laugh. I sober up quickly. "Claudia met with Arturo Rossi to discuss building and renovating several new restaurants."

"Son of a bitch," is her spontaneous reaction.

"I'm sorry. They were frank about keeping you out of the deal. It's not the final proof, but it doesn't look good."

Kendall shakes her head. "I'm so done with all of this. Family or not, if she doesn't have a good explanation, she's out. I've been planning to slim down the company anyway. If she wants to play that way I can put up."

"We should go now, so you can work with Winter and Dunne on strategy."

"What about Dolan?" she asks, her tone soft and warm.

"What about him?" I'm not sure I can deal with this now.

"Did you speak with him?"

"They won't let me," I say grimly. "They have a point. If I'm in the same room with him again, I might kill him. Come on, let's go."

"What did he do?"

I'm taking my chances. At least the surroundings will keep me from having that meltdown that's been in the making since the night we busted him.

"He nearly killed someone I..." Here it comes. I'm choking up. "I cared about."

"My offer still stands," Kendall says, matter-of-factly. "And remember, you have somewhere to go after all of this."

Maybe—but first we'll figure out who's after her. I won't fail this time.

Chapter Twenty-Two

It takes me three calls before I get MacKenzie Winter on the phone. That in itself is worrisome. When I finally get to speak to her, the news isn't reassuring.

"We are a bit swamped right now, just let me get you up to speed." Her tone is tense. "We'll be meeting with the prosecutor's office and Judge Collins this afternoon."

"That's...quick. Any particular reason?"

"We're still trying to figure that out, but it looks like he's going to review the deal and look into making some changes."

"What changes are we talking about? They better not involve prison time."

"We will do our best to avoid that. I'll get back to you."

"Sure. Give me some good news next time. I can use it."

"Kendall." She sounds even more serious all of a sudden. "We are working on this, all right? We're not going to let you down."

"I appreciate that. I'll be waiting for your call."

"I'll call you as soon as I can. Bye."

"Wait a second. Do you have any idea why Lawrence recused herself?"

"Nothing solid. Something about how she might not be able to see this through, some family issues, but I don't know more. Again, we'll talk later."

This time, she ends the call, but I've heard enough.

"Something's not right," I sum up the conversation to Robyn who has just approved our lunch delivery. I join her in the living area. "How much do you know about Judge Lawrence—or Judge Collins for that matter? I know that the latter handled a few cases involving the Biancos."

"I thought that name might be familiar to you," she says as we sit down to eat. "He handled some big anti-corruption cases, and he's about to launch his campaign for governor."

"That's interesting. He and Lawrence make a backdoor deal so he can take over the case and show the public how tough he is on corruption?" It's true, I've heard the name a few times. I don't know enough to judge either way, though I remember Dad saying once that the Biancos get the judges they want. Collins, however, is pretty clear in his agenda, so Tony and his clan were unlucky sometimes?

"Judge Lawrence doesn't strike me as the type to give up cases because of someone else's political aspirations."

"Well, MacKenzie has some meetings this afternoon. After that we'll know more."

"I hope so." Her gaze drifts off, and I wonder if it has to do with the conversation we had earlier. I'm not messing around. It would be a last resort, but still.

"What's on your mind?"

"You could really do that, get us out of town with one phone call?"

"You know I could. You must have had other suspects with connections."

"Believe me, I have. I was just never so tempted."

"I'm tempting you, huh?"

"Right now, food and coffee are still in the running, but...Yes." Okay, it's not going to be a quick seduction, but we still have some time before the call.

"I understand that. They have a pretty good kitchen here, though I can't wait for the day when we can go back to *Catania*."

I'm struck by the longing in her eyes. Her words, however, show that her belief in the shared fantasy is faint.

"I'm not sure if this is ever going to work out. Other agencies are going to investigate after our deal is done. I'm not sure if I can still do my job and keep seeing you after this."

"I thought we had that figured out. After getting shot at numerous times, you'd think a person could get a break. Will they forever question your conduct even after your case is long closed?"

"I don't know." She sounds tired. "Maybe not. But you're one step away from leaving for good, not that I blame you, after everything. To be honest, starting over sounds great, but if there's one thing I'm sure about, it's that I know I can't do it."

She's serious, I can tell.

"I'm sorry to hear that. And I'm sorry you don't think there's much of a chance for us. I understand where you're coming from though."

"Do you?" she asks, her tone between hopeful and resigned.

"Listen, I never even thought I'd have a relationship beyond the occasional inconsequential one-night stand. I worked day and night to prove myself, to my parents who obviously kept a lot of secrets, to the rest of my family. Where that leaves me now...I guess you know that better than anyone else. I have to pick up the pieces, and I know you might not be able to be there for it, but you're here now. Do you trust me?"

"What, you're thinking of something kinky?" Robyn asks, amused.

That didn't cross my mind before, though it does now. Stick to the plan.

"I might be at some point, but right now, all I'm asking you is to work with me. I want to take you out tonight. I promise it will be safe, far away from any potential and real killers."

I expected the caution in her expression.

"That's risky. My boss needs to know where we are...and you're awaiting a pretty important phone call."

"I promise we are not making a run for it. It's just dinner, I swear." And maybe an overnight stay, if nothing out of the ordinary happens, but I don't want to freak her out. "I wouldn't do anything risky."

She snorts.

"Yes, okay, I admit I could have handled Claudia in a different manner. That story isn't over yet. I want to find out what she's doing with Arturo. But I need a break desperately, and I think you need it too. We'll keep in touch with everyone. Just one evening." At this point I'm pleading. I need this to work. Because I want to get my will, but also because this might be my last chance for a great gesture, depending on where the judge is going with this.

"One evening."

"Yes, that's all I'm asking."

"We're going to *Catania*?"

"No, not this time. I'm just going to make a few calls, and we'll be good to go."

"I guess I'll do the same then."

I reach out to touch her cheek. "This will be good." Then I get up to go to the bedroom where I make a quick call to Claudia. I'm not going to confront her yet.

"You snuck away to call me?" she asks, amused. "Is she paying attention at all?"

"Leave it. I just need to ask you a quick question."

"Still didn't hire the hitman. Really, that's the only lead the FBI has? Pathetic."

"Claudia. Do you remember Uncle Lorenzo, or Luca, ever talking about Judge Collins?"

"A couple of times, why?"

"You think he was friendly with the Biancos?"

"Oh, no, I don't think so. Some of their henchmen got pretty hefty sentences a few years ago. Why are you...oh. I see. Be careful, I guess. He's looking to lock some people up before running for governor."

"Okay. Thanks for the warning."

"I mean it, be careful. I might not be happy with some of your decisions, but I don't want you to go to prison either." She sighs. "Much as I hate to say it, you were right about Luca. He made his bed."

"I'll talk to you later."

"I guess your lawyers will make sure things stay on track."

"I'll hear from them later today. Wish me luck."

My next call is to the number my father provided, another last resort, though this will be more of a compromise. Robyn can't afford to disappear, and neither can I. There is too much work to do.

I call and relate my wishes. The person on the other end of the line is 100% professional. They ask the questions I expected, about some details in family history that only a few people know. I give all the right answers. After my identity is established the conversation switches to my needs for tonight.

"This won't be long-term, Ms. Mancini?" the woman clarifies.

No, definitely not long-term. One night only.

"No," I say. "A week at the most."

"Very well."

"And something else—I need to be sure that the privacy of the place will be safeguarded beyond that time."

"Of course, Ms. Mancini. We will take every necessary measure."

"Thank you."

"My pleasure."

The car will arrive an hour from now. Time to get ready.

Chapter
Twenty-Three

I still can't tell whether Kendall is taking all the recent news exceptionally well, or not so well at all.

"No," I say when she's starting to pack clothes into a suitcase. "This is not what we agreed on."

"It's a place with formal attire," she says, unfazed. "We have a small trip ahead, and I don't want to dress up yet."

"Why do I feel like I am going to regret this?"

"You won't," she promises. "You're all set with your colleagues?"

I can't say that at all. But tomorrow, things might be very different if Judge Collins is questioning the deal, and I have a hard time saying no to Kendall. A part of me is still surprised that in the midst of all this, a nice dinner with me is her priority. Formal attire.

"What if I don't have anything to wear?"

"You'll be fine. Better yet, let me take care of it. We'll have someone pick us up in an hour, and we'll be back here sooner than you think. No one will be the wiser. Please?"

I shouldn't.

I'm curious.

"All right." Beyond this, I might not be able to do much for her, if Dad is right. I did my own research into Judge Collins, and him taking over the case is likely to signal tougher times for Kendall—even given the list of good deeds she's done. But I think this conversation can wait until after dinner.

———

"What is this?" I ask when the driver parks on the curb and steps outside to open the door for us.

"What I told you. We're going to dinner. Ethan here is going to drive us."

"Ethan." I cast a suspicious look at the man wearing a black uniform—rather non-descript, but from a fabric that looks expensive.

"Don't worry, Agent Johnson. I can assure you our clients' safety and satisfaction are our highest priority."

Which one, I almost ask. There's only one priority.

"This is a private service for people who need a bit of a getaway," Kendall explains. "Think of it as a pre-paid package. Dad invested some money so that if someone in the family ever wanted to use it, they could."

I'm not sure if that's good enough. "That's not an emergency. How easy to infiltrate?"

Ethan looks a tad insulted at that.

"Very hard to do so," she says cheerily. "After all this, do you think I want to get shot again? I want to have good food and drinks in peace, and for one evening forget about what might happen tomorrow. Get in the damn car."

I do. Maybe I'm a little stunned by all this. I'd like to think that my instincts are still on the money. I'll let her have this—me—for tonight.

We drive about fifteen minutes, leaving the city lights behind.

"Don't worry, that's all in the plan. He's not going to slit anyone's throat." Kendall, back in control, is enjoying this way too much.

"Ma'am," Ethan mumbles, clearly not feeling the joke.

"Sorry about that. Agent Johnson is a bit jumpy. For a good reason, but this will all go well, right? Their reviews on, what is it? Shout? Gasp? They're all five stars."

I can't help it. I have to laugh. "Somehow I don't think this is a service you'd find on a public Internet site."

"You would be right about that." Ethan sounds relieved.

"We'll be fine," Kendall says as she takes my hand.

That, however, is still to be determined when we drive up to what looks like a private hangar. All of a sudden, her packing a couple of different outfits for a fancy dinner makes a lot more sense.

"Kendall, no. You promised me."

"That we're not going to make a run for it. We're not. I'm sorry my plan of taking you to the cabin went so wrong last time. I understand I didn't take the right precautions, and I didn't know Jimmy was about to go off the rails. This is different. I swear to you."

"Where are we going? You know you cannot leave the country."

"No one's leaving the country. We'll go on a short plane ride, then we can change and have dinner. If anything, we're safer than we were as sitting ducks in that hotel room."

She does have a point—as long as everyone working for this luxury service plays along.

"You're dipping into the college fund."

"I guess I am. I learned something from all of this—if you wait too long, you might regret it."

I suppress the shudder. I know the truth behind this all too well.

"Okay. *Carpe diem*. Let's do it."

"You will not regret it."

I'm more aware than most people where and how the rich hide away their money, especially when they do it illegally. I knew that even with the legal part of the Mancini Group and Adria, there's a lot of money involved, and a lot of money has been in the Mancini family for generations.

So Alphonso managed to take some precautions for his wife, daughter and himself. My jaw still drops when we walk up to the property topped by a dome, columns framing the entrance. There's a fountain in front, and a magnificent staircase leading to the front door. A king's summerhouse.

"Yeah, I know it's big, but we have state-of-the-art security," Kendall informs me.

I don't remind her that we've seen in the past weeks that there can always be glitches.

"It's beautiful," I have to admit. "That's the college fund? A fortress in case the authorities or rival families get too close?"

The gaze she gives me borders on sympathetic. "It's for a small getaway. If anyone came too close for my comfort, we'd be in a different place already. I know you thought I was foolish with Claudia, but I don't take that kind of chance."

"Good to know. I'd still like to check the place."

"Sure, I expected that. I'll go with you. After that, we can change and go to the restaurant."

"Where will that be?"

"It's on the property," she says with a shrug. "Let's get this over with so we can get to the fun part?"

"Sounds good to me."

Kendall unlocks the door, and we step inside what looks like a bit of an understated fairy tale castle.

Fit for a princess—I can't help being amused remembering the nickname everyone from the authorities to rival family members uses. I imagine it originally came from her parents who created this getaway oasis. Including a restaurant. It's unreal.

I focus on the task at hand, checking each room Kendall shows me with pride. I understand now why she had us come early. This will take a while.

"You've never been here? No pictures even?"

"No, I'm seeing this for the first time, just as you are. It's pretty amazing if a bit remote. Not that I worry," she clarifies quickly. "It would be tricky to work from here."

"I got you." This has more than one meaning as we walk through each room, sitting rooms, bedrooms, baths, kitchens—yes, more than one. I familiarize myself with the security system. I've come across that brand before. It's not cheap, but worth every cent I've been told.

"I know. Staff has been vetted, and I hope you don't want to look at their résumés now. I'd like to go change and then start with a cocktail."

Satisfied with what I've seen, I nod, and she directs me back to one of the bedrooms.

This kind of luxury is obscene. The four-poster bed dominates the room, matching furniture include nightstands and a sitting area with armchairs by a window made from bulletproof glass.

"I know what you're thinking. But I promise you, not all of my money goes to frivolous fun. And tonight?

I don't regret any cent that goes to it." Kendall steps behind me.

"I need to take a shower." Really, that's the first thing I say out loud?

"In a moment." She kisses my neck, warm hands stealing underneath my shirt. "I mean it. I want you to enjoy tonight."

"I will." I have no doubts. No need for any more words when her curious fingers sneak under the fabric of my bra. It's dangerous. It's unavoidable.

"Do you want to come in the shower with me?" I turn to her, seeing her eyes darken with desire. I guess I have my answer.

In the spacious bathroom, we quickly strip, leaving clothes all over the tiled floor. Once we're naked under the hot stream, Kendall pulls me into a close embrace, the intimate contact melting away a lot of the tension from the past days. She pours some shampoo into her hands and gestures for me to turn around. The relaxing effect of her hands in my hair, gently massaging, is exquisite. At the same time, another kind of tension grips my body. She replaces shampoo with shower gel, exploring me with warm, slick hands. I can't keep any secret from her touch. Any movement is to give her more access, to show my appreciation—to finally let go. Kendall is patient, waiting until I have caught my breath, holding me until my legs are a bit steadier.

I get to my knees, looking up at her, finding nothing but anticipation in her expression.

I won't disappoint her either.

REDEMPTION

With the job comes a lot of ugliness. Someone has to do it, I used to shrug it off, but being confronted with, and enveloped by this much beauty, art, architecture, sex...being with her...I am more aware of it than ever. And I'll dig hard to find good reasons to go back to it, beyond "someone has to do it." I am tired. It's something Kendall saw the moment we met, and she cut right through my defenses and excuses. It's nothing I can dwell on right now, because we're getting ready to go to the bar.

Kendall is putting on a red dress while I go for more comfortable slacks. I hope the shiny green top will do.

"Perfect," she says when I put my hair into a ponytail, and I scoff.

The nickname princess didn't stick for nothing. Here, hidden away with me, she does her hair and make-up fit for a gala, and she does it effortlessly.

"Don't make that face. I mean it. Let's have a drink."

The restaurant is situated directly under the dome, the bar located in the center of it. It's smaller than the Adria locations, smaller than *Catania* even, because obviously it's not meant for a big group. We checked it earlier, but it's even more impressive now that it's dark.

"Your dad had quite the imagination," I say. "I assume he chose the décor and everything."

Kendall shakes her head with a wistful smile.

"I have no idea when he had the time to do this, but I appreciate it. Good evening," she says to the bartender, a woman in her mid-twenties. "Anything the lady wants, and...Surprise me."

"Absolutely," the woman returns cheerily. "What can I get you?"

"A Manhattan, please."

"Coming right up."

I look behind me, taking in the tables arranged along the windows of the circular room, the amazing views.

"When all of this is over, I will remember I've had the best food and drinks of my life."

"Not just that, I hope." Kendall's smug smile tells me without a doubt what she is thinking of.

"No, not just that. The sex was pretty good too." The bartender returns with our drinks, a Manhattan for me, a yellow-orange-red ombre concoction for Kendall. Serves me right. She doesn't bat an eye though.

"No need to use past tense yet."

While the implications make me squirm just a bit in anticipation, I have to keep a clear head, as much as that is possible.

"We have to go back tonight."

"MacKenzie hasn't gotten back to me yet. There is no urgency."

"What if they want to meet in the morning? What if Judge Collins has planned something?"

"It will all still be there tomorrow. We'll fly back early in the morning."

"Are you scared?" Maybe the question should be, aren't you scared? Kendall takes a few seconds too long for my liking.

"I didn't have much time to think about it. Perhaps I've been stalling to face it all, but if you want to know the truth, I'm okay with stalling a little while longer. Right now, I'm just grateful that my parents created this opportunity for me. And I think our table is ready."

Walking the few steps to the table I ponder her words. I might be projecting. Is it me who's scared, for letting my guard down this much? It's highly unlikely that anything will happen during this getaway, and maybe that's not even the point. I've gotten to know her a little, but she keeps teasing and toying with me, and I keep coming back for more. How much longer can we do this?

There's no menu—the evening starts with an excellent wine and a smoked salmon appetizer course.

Halfway through, Kendall apologizes when her cell phone rings, my heart beating faster when she says, "Well, I'll have to talk to MacKenzie about her timing." She half turns away. "Hi. Yes, I can talk." She listens with an impassive expression, not giving me anything. I can't help thinking how different this is from only moments ago, when she was completely open to me. Business-woman, head of the family Kendall Mancini is still very different from Kendall, my lover.

That's a startling thought.

"All right, I guess we'll work with that," she says curtly and ends the call.

"How did it go?"

"Just a quick update." Kendall picks up her glass. "Seems like the deal will hold, but MacKenzie wants a meeting with your people tomorrow afternoon. They'll get back to us soon. See, you didn't need to worry. We don't have to be there early."

"You always win, don't you?" There's mostly admiration and a bit of jealousy in my tone. Once upon a time, I thought I'd be so good at this. Perhaps I'd met criminals who weren't half as smart, and never before did I fall in love to the point that the term criminal felt wrong. Kendall cares about people other than herself. Attached to the Mancini Group is the foundation dedicated to empowering women business owners, and women's rights at home and all the partner countries. That's something, right?

"I just want to do my best, and not forget that others are less fortunate. That's how I was raised."

We do have a lot in common, Kendall and me. It's still unclear what conclusions we'll draw from that fact.

Chapter Twenty-Four

I don't want Robyn to worry. In fact, I wanted to create an environment where she'd be comfortable—maybe comfortable enough to talk to me about Dolan, and what the plan is. It could still happen. For that, I had to bend the truth a little. I hate to be distracted, but MacKenzie's report was worrisome. When the chef prepares dessert and coffee for us, I excuse myself and call her again. This has to stop. I hate making calls from bathrooms.

"What are we going to do about him?" I ask without preamble. It's not fine. In fact, Judge Collins is a disaster for us, as he wants to shake up the deal.

"Slow down, Kendall, there's not much we can do at the moment. Our in-house investigator is on it, but it's early."

"He's had some run-ins with the Biancos. Check Arturo Rossi as well."

"Thanks for the tip."

Did that sound sarcastic? I pay her too much to scoff at me.

"You have to admit, the timing is curious."

"It is, but we know that he's preparing to run, and he wants a strong argument. That might be all."

"I don't feel altruistic enough to help with his campaign. What points could he make?"

"For one, he wants to look at Luca as well. I need to know if he has something on you that he might be willing to trade."

"Luca? You can't be serious. He was the one doing the drug deals."

"Does he?"

"I don't think so."

"Okay. I'll talk to you tomorrow. If we find anything in the meantime, I'll text you."

The door opens and Robyn walks in.

"Hey!"

"Everything all right?" MacKenzie asks, alarmed.

"No, it's all good, just the agent walking in on me in the bathroom."

"I didn't need to know that."

"Not the time for jokes, MacKenzie. Talk to you tomorrow."

I end the call and look at Robyn who's leaning against the door, studying me. Her posture and expression scream frustration and resignation. I can see her point. I'm frustrated with myself. In this network of who does what for whom, of course judges are involved. Uncle Lorenzo might have been a bigot, but he wouldn't actively work against someone else in the family. It seems that with my generation, all bets are off. Yes, I wore that wire and got Luca arrested. It was the right thing to do—wasn't it?

"And now I can never pee in peace again. Say it."

"Say what? That I can't trust you? That you're lying to me whenever you feel like it? I know that already."

That stings. "I was trying not to spoil the evening, but since you're asking for it—Judge Collins is bad news.

He's looking for ways to sabotage the deal, because he thinks it got too sweet for me."

"Did it?" she asks. "What do you think you deserve?"

"I don't know. What everyone deserves. Peace?"

We leave the bathroom to go back to the table, and when our dessert arrives, I order another bottle of wine. Who cares anymore?

"You always thought I got off too easily, didn't you?"

"Part of me did, maybe," she admits. "The other part remembers that you risked your life to save me. That's very unlike someone in your line of business."

"It's not unlike the values I was taught. You stake your claim, you protect what's yours—but you don't step on someone who's already down."

"Judge Collins isn't the only player in this. The prosecutors were fine with the deal."

"He can always go beyond their recommendation." I pour a glass for each of us and drink deeply from mine. "I'm really sorry. I wanted this to turn out a different way, and...I guess I am scared. Not so much of going to prison, but of finding out who I really am."

"That's tough on everyone, believe me."

"Not you though. You figured it out."

She shakes her head with a laugh. "I thought I had. Before."

"Dolan?"

"I was going to say, before you, but you have a point. Anyway, that's over, with him I mean. During that hostage crisis, he nearly killed someone who meant a lot to me, and it wasn't because he didn't want to. Backup arrived in time, but it was..." She takes a shaky breath and refills her glass. "Close."

"I'm sorry. Could he still be a threat?"

"No. Hampton and Carr assured me it's under control. It's partly the reason why they assigned me to you, because they didn't want me there."

"So, it's not just to torture you."

She chuckles. "I don't think so. All this food and booze—I've really fallen on hard times, haven't I?"

I don't go for the distraction though. "That colleague of yours, were you together?"

The answer seems obvious, but she still has a surprise left.

"If it had been up to me...I wanted it, but I wasn't out, and she wasn't...available. Or gay. It shouldn't matter. All this was just a complete nightmare. She left the FBI and moved away. Last thing I heard she got married, so there's that. But I still remember what that fear felt like—that she could die. Or any of us in that room."

"Jimmy, Bianco, all of that must have brought up a lot of memories."

"No kidding. I was close to taking you up on that offer. Even now...This is someone who has killed, and more than we even know with the drug trade. I don't know anyone who'd miss him, but there should be boundaries, right?"

"He's behind bars. That's something."

We are both silent for moments that stretch into minutes. I hold up the bottle.

"You'd like to take this upstairs?"

"I'd love to."

—ele—

Whatever happens from now on, I won't regret taking her here. What I wanted to show her, what I needed to see for myself is that something resembling a safe place still exists—and that she can be here with me. It feels good to be ignorant of the realistic dangers, of all responsibility—of plans for the future that might never come true. Instead, I get to make love to her in decadent luxurious surroundings, lost in the ebb and flow of resist and surrender. Robyn might be right to think she can never fully trust me. I have too many secrets, too many obligations.

But she can be safe with me right here and now, and that's not something either of us takes lightly.

I focus all my attention on her, the sensation of her warm skin under my hands and lips, and still, the thought crosses my mind...

I won't go to prison. If Judge Collins decides that should be the case, the last resort option is still available.

We fall asleep entwined, the covers pulled haphazardly over our bodies.

The sound of a cell phone rouses us much too soon. It's Robyn's. She doesn't have a good enough poker face—I can instantly tell the news is bad.

"What the fuck is wrong with people?" she curses, the words sounding even harsher in the still of the night. "I can't believe this. Yes, we are safe. I'll call you back."

"That doesn't sound good."

"Because it's not," she says darkly, tossing the phone onto the nightstand. "Someone detonated a small device in the hotel room. No one was hurt, but it's a mess in there."

"Oh. I feel even better about whisking you away to this place now."

"Don't get ahead of yourself. We have to get back. Dolan is out."

"What?"

I immediately think that I could make a particular call right this moment. This won't be a recurring nightmare for her. I'll make sure of that.

"No one understands it. He must have turned on someone higher up, but even then..."

"Who signed off on this? Collins?"

"Judge Lawrence did."

"You think she's dirty too?"

Robyn gets out of bed and starts dressing. Reluctantly, I do the same. I understand the urgency to take action, though where to start?

"I'm not sure," she answers my question. "I wouldn't rule out that she's been pressured into it. By whom? I don't know. But if this is connected, and Dolan got out while Collins wants to lock you up, there's one person at the center of it."

"Luca," I say, feeling exhausted all of a sudden. "I guess I should pay him that visit."

The gaze she gives me is almost sympathetic. "That wouldn't be the worst idea. I suppose that plane is on standby, or do we have to drive all the way?"

"I'll make the call."

Our little getaway is without a doubt over. We're back to damage control. Claudia and Arturo, Luca and Dolan, this will all make sense soon. It has to, so we can finally be free.

Chapter
Twenty-Five

Approximately two hours later, I stand in front of what's left of the door, staring at the destruction. Part of me is in shock. The person who did this wasn't sending a warning—they wanted both of us dead.

Wearing shoe covers and gloves, I step over the threshold to take a closer look at the scene.

Kendall is in Rachel Carr's office now, and she won't go anywhere until the meeting with her lawyers. I had to come here and see it for myself.

"That gives us a new avenue," I say to Hampton who has come up behind me. "I don't think Claudia Mancini has the contacts to get explosives?"

"She might know somebody who does. Also, Dolan could be a candidate."

"That's fast. He just got out."

I had the same thought though. He and Luca might have tried to implicate Kendall, and...then what? Judge Collins just went for it? "How did that happen anyway? You got any new information on that?"

"Not much. He and Lawrence had a meeting a day before she recused herself from Ms. Mancini's case."

"And that's not a red flag?"

"He helped put some of Bianco's henchmen away, but..."

"What?" I press.

"I don't want to speculate. There's a lot we don't know. I can't see the judge trying to blow up a hotel room. He's been very vocal about trying to curb corruption."

"So, he makes sure Dolan gets out? I'm sure Lawrence didn't come up with that idea out of the blue."

"Let's not make accusations yet," he suggests. "What about you? It took you a while to get here."

"Kendall took me to dinner," I say with a last look at the burned room, suppressing a shudder.

Kendall, who organized a luxury getaway within an hour. What did I miss? Did she know something like this was coming? As I follow Hampton outside the room, something springs to mind.

"What about Luca Mancini, or Claudia? Did they have any prior connections with either one of those judges?"

"We are looking into it right now." His gaze is serious when he ads, "This has taken a turn. I'm glad you're okay."

"Thanks. Me too."

I catch a ride back to the office with Hampton and use the time to make a call.

"Hey Dad, I don't have much time, but maybe you could help me with something. Did you ever hear Alphonso say anything about certain judges? And were you aware of any member of the Mancini family working with Arturo Rossi behind the other ones' backs?"

"Wow, all of this before my first coffee. I assume you know the Mancinis had no lost love for Rossi after they rescued his daughter from the Bianco clan. I never heard anything of the kind, but anything is possible."

I want to tear my hair out. I can't blame him. After all he's enjoying his well-deserved retirement. We need a break. We need to figure out who wants Kendall dead.

"As for the other thing, yes, I remember Al saying that the Biancos got a sweet deal all the time. Some of their foot soldiers were put away, but cases against Tony and his sons often fell apart, no matter the evidence. Why?"

"Did he mention anyone in particular?"

Hampton keeps his eyes on the road, but I can tell he's curious.

"I don't think so. You wouldn't ask me that if you didn't have a suspicion?" I decide to take my chances. "The judge on Kendall's case recused himself, and in came an anti-corruption crusader." This time, Hampton shoots me a quizzical glance, making me cringe. Yes, I know that sounds bad, coming from someone like me. There's a context. "Which wouldn't be a bad thing, but I wonder if rooting out corruption is all that's on his agenda. He's had run-ins with the Biancos, and like you said, it never got to the top."

"There could be many reasons for that," he reminds me. "Lack of evidence...I'm sure everyone involved did what they could. That was the whole point of getting close to the Mancinis, because we had mutual interests."

"Okay, thank you, Dad. Talk to you later."

"An anti-corruption crusader," Hampton repeats my words after I've ended the call.

"You have to admit it's a strange coincidence."

"And maybe that's all it is, a coincidence. Lawrence cited family issues. You can't predict these."

"She had time to let Dolan out."

He doesn't argue with that. "Still, Collins? He's on the conservative side, impeccable record. If he says someone should take another look at that deal, maybe he's right."

"You thought Kendall should have gone to prison all along."

"I think," he says calmly, "she helped us a lot. She, and maybe her parents, too, had good intentions, and they have put some money in the right places. Unfortunately, they withheld a lot of money from the government, and that is no joke. I just don't see how she's aware of any wrongdoing."

Is she? I think of the getaway, dinner turning into a decadent night, and before that, her meeting with Claudia, involving Sofia to distract me while she was investigating the "college fund."

Kendall is as irresistible as she is elusive. I'd be a fool to think one or the other would ever change.

"And I don't think you're completely objective in this."

"That's low." That's exactly the truth, but I haven't slept enough, and I only learned a few hours ago that someone tried to blow us up. "I want to find who's after her so we can close the damn case."

Hampton shakes his head. "She's Kendall Mancini. Someone is always going to be after her."

"So we should just let them?"

"I didn't say that. What I meant is that she might be safer in prison, considering that person got into her home and the hotel."

"Yeah, what the hell is up with that? We've been vetting the kitchen, her security personnel, and still..." An idea is forming. It might be even crazier than anything I've done before, but at this point we have to think outside the box. Traditional measures haven't gotten us very far. Kendall's is no ordinary case. We might have to go for extraordinary.

REDEMPTION

ele

Hampton and I sit in Rachel's office for an update when Ryan comes rushing in.

"This is going to get us a warrant for Rossi," she says triumphantly, holding up a sheet of paper.

I take the paper from her, whistling through my teeth. Rossi is in real estate as well, but the timing of him signing off on an order of explosives is curious.

"Finally good news. I'd like to have a shot at him."

"You better get going on this," Rachel warns. "We have the meeting with Judge Collins at 4:00 p.m. sharp."

"Nothing I'd rather do," I say grimly. "We have a good chance, too, to get to the bottom of Claudia Mancini's involvement in this mess."

"Okay. Why are you still here?"

ele

Arturo Rossi is like most of the criminal men I've met in my career, cocky, threatening endless expensive lawsuits, *indignant* that someone might try to hold him accountable. There are too many connections to ignore, Claudia Mancini, the explosives. I feel pretty good when we knock on his door to arrest him.

"You will regret this," he claims.

"We'll see about that, but it's about time we talk."

Rossi scoffs at that, though he doesn't resist when the other agents lead him down the front steps of his impressive mansion, and to the car. I watch them drive away, hoping I did the right thing.

I have a plan. I wish I could have a good long talk with Kendall before we set it in motion, but it's for the better.

Her wellbeing and that of the public is more important than my own sensibilities.

I can do this.

I will need a lot more caffeine to get through the next few days.

"Coffee first," I say when we get back to the office.

"You're sure you should be doing this?" Hampton still has doubts. I have no use for them right now.

"I am. It's about time we put a stop to all of it."

Rossi's lawyer has materialized, and we all sit down.

"This is absolutely preposterous," Dorman, the Rossis' family attorney, claims. "My client has no ties to Ms. Mancini. He wishes her no harm either."

"This isn't your signature?"

Rossi scans the sheet, shaking his head. "It sure looks like it, but what would I do with this amount of explosives? That's not exactly my business."

"You want to tell us there's no ill will toward the Mancinis from your side—like the long-held grudge for getting your daughter away from Frank Bianco?"

"She's still telling that story? Sofia ran away and embarrassed me. That was a long time ago. I have enough on my plate with my son being in jail, set up by my so-called friend Tony. No, I'm done with all of this. Sofia can do whatever the hell she pleases, and so can Kendall."

This is a bit surprising, to say the least. He might just be that good an actor.

"You have no explanation for how that signature ended up on this purchase."

"My client already told you!" I'm not impressed with Dorman's bluster.

"You must admit it's curious. I don't assume that happens often?"

"That people try to screw with me?" Rossi scoffs. "All the time."

"I'm so sorry to hear that. What does that mean, you are in need of allies? Someone like Claudia Mancini? We know you've been working on a project with her."

"So? It's not illegal."

"It is when you're plotting murder on the side."

"Agent! That is unacceptable."

"Is it? I'd think that both you and your client have an interest in clearing this up as soon as possible. If Mr. Rossi didn't sign the purchase order, who had access? Who did sign that order? You've been walking a fine line for many years now. You must have an idea."

"I'm not a rat, and I'm not going to do your job for you."

"Fine." I shrug. "But you might have heard that Judge Collins is on the case now, and he's looking at all the connections. Might be a shame if you turned out to be collateral damage, no?"

"Whatever Kendall did, I have nothing to do with it. Let him do whatever he wants to do."

"Arturo." There's a hint of warning to Dorman's tone. We might be on to something.

"Agent Johnson, I'll need a few minutes with my client."

"Of course." I get to my feet and nod to Hampton. "We'll be back. I hope you make the right choice, Mr. Rossi."

Chapter Twenty-Six

"**Y**ou don't like me," I observe. It's something to pass the time. I'm cautious, concerned...and bored.

Ryan Farmer gives me a wry shrug. "I don't reserve any special resentment for you."

That's more honest than I expected her to be.

"Just the usual, then?"

"You are incredibly lucky, Ms. Mancini."

"Yet I'm here hanging out with the FBI, hiding from a stalker turned bomber when I'd much rather have a long, tedious day at work."

Perhaps she doesn't consider what I do, or used to do day to day, work, but she's gracious enough not to say it.

"Don't worry," I add. "I'm alive and not in jail. Believe me, I'm counting my blessings."

"Good. You still have no idea who's behind this?"

"The bombing? No. There was an incident once at one of my father's sites, but we chalked it up to an accident. Nothing could be proven."

She frowns. "Why haven't we learned this before?"

"I'm telling you now. It was nothing. Accidents happen."

"A lot of unexplained incidents have happened around your family. Did you ever report it?"

"I'm sure my father did. What are you saying, that the same person is doing this now?"

She shrugs. "You seem very nonchalant about all of it. You care a lot about Agent Johnson, don't you?"

Okay, I can see where this is coming from.

"I do, and I'm aware, so do all of her colleagues. I wouldn't do anything to endanger her life if that's what you're implying. Unless you are insinuating something else."

Like I said, I'm cautious. Bored. I wish Robyn and I could go back to the oasis. We had peace for a few hours.

"Like what?"

"Are you jealous?"

Agent Farmer laughs. "I'm married."

"That's not the answer to my question."

"You want an answer, I think it's sad that we need to allocate resources babysitting you right now. You got the sweetest deal ever out of this, and you live your life like nothing has changed."

Oh, she and Hampton are on the same page.

"That's not exactly true. A lot has changed. I lost my parents. Pretty much everyone I relied on, turned on me, and I'm trying to run a clean business. Or at least, that's what I would do if I wasn't stuck here."

"Well, things might be changing."

I wait for more of an explanation, but she doesn't give me any.

"Will they? What do you mean by that?"

"I can't tell you more at this time. We all have to wait and see."

I suppose that has to do with the judge and the conclusions he will draw. All in all, not a good prospect.

"You think there's a way to get lunch somewhere around here?"

Her expression is somewhere between resigned and surprised.

"What? We didn't have breakfast after you called in the middle of the night. So?"

With a sigh, she gets up. "I'll get you something," she promises.

I wonder why Robyn hasn't checked in once.

—*ell*—

Winter and Dunne have it covered, right? At least I hope so. I did what I had to do, cooperate, clean up the part of the business that wasn't entirely clean. I still have to oversee the sale of Adria. There's a lot of work to be done, and I can't be sitting on my hands just because someone has it in them for me.

Time is ticking by. I'm starting to get worried, and not just because of my lunch.

What would it take for Robyn to tell all about the special service we enjoyed the other night? No, she wouldn't do that. But there's something curious about this recent occurrence, and Ryan Farmer's theory that the bombing could be connected to the earlier incident on a construction site.

Did I, or did Dad overlook the signs for that long? I can't have all those additional complications, not when I'm waiting for Judge Collins' verdict on the deal. Can it still be saved? If not, what does that mean for me...and for Robyn, the two of us?

The door opens, but instead of Agent Farmer, Robyn enters.

"Thank God. I was starting to worry you'd just leave me here. We will go to another hotel I assume?"

"I'm afraid that's not possible," she says, sounding tired. I realize that she's also carrying a take-out bag with her. "Ryan said you were hungry. Let's talk."

"Sure. You have a lead? Anything to do with Dolan, or Judge Collins?"

She starts putting food on the table, plates and utensils. My stomach growls at the expected delicacies.

"Let's have lunch first."

"And then what? Will you talk to me?"

"I'm sorry, Kendall. New evidence has come up, and...we'll have to take you into custody."

"You're kidding me."

"I'm afraid I'm not. I have no choice. This is the best I could do."

I thought the day couldn't get any worse when I learned that someone had blown up the hotel suite. I realize I was sadly mistaken.

Chapter Twenty-Seven

I can tell Kendall is shell-shocked. Still hungry, though, I assume from the way she absent-mindedly eats her food.

"No. This can't be happening. I thought things were under control. Someone tried to blow me, us, up, and you want to arrest me? What, you think I did it?"

"No one thinks that," I say patiently. "This is not related."

"It's ridiculous, that's what it is. I want to talk to my lawyers now."

"That will be arranged."

I'm calm and in control, on the surface. It's an odd state to be in. I know I'm on the right track, doing the right thing. It feels terrible at the same time because I know she's scared for real. We'll have to isolate her, because otherwise, prison would pose a different kind of threat.

For now, we have to focus on the crimes that have happened on the outside, in order to avoid the worst-case scenario.

"I never thought you'd do that."

"Do what? I have no choice."

"You do," she says. I can't blame her for the bitter tone of her voice. "You know you do. I gave you a taste of it...but you have to be a goody two-shoes? Right? Perhaps deep down you think you don't deserve anything good, maybe it's because of what happened to your friend. I am not like that. I'm not going to take the blame for everyone's bullshit."

"Okay."

"Okay? What does that mean?"

Her words have a surprising impact, hitting close to home. It's important that we stay on track. "If you're ready...?"

"I'm not ready," she snaps. "You didn't think to bring me fortune cookies? Wait, I know what it would say. *Trust no one.*"

"Kendall. We have to go."

By we, I mean Kendall, and the agents who will deliver her, because I have a lot of work to do now.

Claudia Mancini agrees to come in and talk to me without a second of hesitation. An hour after I left Kendall, her cousin sits across from me, looking all too relaxed given the recent turmoil in her family.

"I'm happy to help," she says, "though I'm not sure how. By now you are probably aware that Kendall tells a lot of stories, most of them to make herself look good—better in comparison, anyway. And no, I had no idea about Luca's dealings, but I told you guys a million times already. What else?"

"This doesn't have anything to do with Luca or Kendall."

She raises an eyebrow but doesn't comment.

"Do you remember an incident on one of the Mancini group's sites a few years ago? An explosion?"

Claudia frowns. "I can't say I do...wait. Maybe. This is what you asked me here for? I have no idea who did it. If I remember correctly, it was an accident. No one got hurt."

"You started an interesting new project recently, with Mr. Rossi."

She doesn't deny it.

"I know he was *persona non grata* for Kendall, and her parents, but it's good business. Someone has to remember that now that she's losing the reins. I mean, look at all that drama. She's not going to last."

"You want to make it happen faster?" I'm aware of the sharp tone of my voice. Claudia's smirk tells me she's noticed it too.

"It's not up to me. Kendall has made so many mistakes, she's in over her head. I'm not saying Luca was smart to do what he did, but he would have made better choices if she had given him a chance."

"Really? I thought his chances were limited because his father couldn't imagine a gay man running things."

"Say what you want, but Kendall will go down at some point. And someone has to pick up the slack. Looks like it's going to be me, and I'm not going to sit out a great opportunity because the guy delivering it to me is a misogynist asshole."

"Well said. There's just one problem."

"That would be?"

"The misogynist asshole is trying to take you down with him."

Claudia sits up straighter. I hold her gaze, waiting.

"Is that a kind of bluff they teach you in FBI school? Wow. I know Arturo isn't a good guy. He knows I don't like him. Hell, nobody likes him. He's in it for the money and so am I."

"He ordered explosives, just like the ones that were on that site. He claims he didn't sign off on that order, and the only other person who wants Kendall out of the way as much as he does is...you, Claudia."

"That's bullshit. I have never killed anyone or ordered a hit. I wouldn't start now. I can do this better than the princess, and I don't need actions like that to prove it. All I need is a freaking chance!"

She sounds pretty sincere, but I'm not here to help her with her issues.

"So you didn't forge Arturo's signature."

"Of course I didn't."

How's that great deal with the misogynist asshole working out for you now?

"Do I need to speak to my lawyer?"

That is something she, Kendall and everyone in those families have in common. There's nothing much amusing about the situation, but still—it's so predictable.

"You can do that, of course, but maybe you can help us and put yourself in a much better situation. Right now, it's Arturo's word against yours. He told us you promised to take care of Kendall, and that you both knew what that meant."

Claudia shakes her head. "He's delusional. Okay, I am questioning my choices. Send my apologies to Sofia, he is much more of an asshole than I thought. All I wanted was my share while Kendall was lounging in that hotel room with you, doing whatever, but definitely not taking care of business."

"It was not her choice."

"Is that my problem, really? You must have something you want, so let's just cut to the chase. What is it? Who do you want me to turn on?"

I ignore the accusation. She's in no position to be indignant about anything.

"We are mainly interested in Arturo and his connections. Tell me about those dinners your dad had with him and Judge Collins."

I can see realization dawn on her face.

"Oh, that's clever. You wanted to scare me first."

"I want the truth," I shoot back. "Every minute you're stalling, you're making things more difficult for you."

Claudia leans back in her chair, her expression still too smug for my liking.

"An FBI agent desperate to find dirt on a judge with a spotless reputation. I wonder how that happened."

The tension in the room is at an uncomfortable high.

"You are in trouble, Claudia."

"So are you, Agent Johnson—but this might be your lucky day."

~ele~

I go back to the room where Arturo is still waiting with his lawyer. He isn't so cocky anymore.

"I'm not telling you a damn thing," he says. "Lock me up if you want, I don't care. It's better than being a rat. It's better than being dead."

His concerns aren't completely unwarranted, I have to give him that.

"There are ways to protect you."

"You can't protect me. This is much bigger than a family rivalry."

The door opens, and Rachel Carr steps inside.

"There's a window here, Mr. Rossi. It's about to close. We know that your son was handed a raw deal, and that Frank Bianco was involved in this. But he wasn't the only one, was he?"

Arturo stares back at her. He isn't budging.

"You signed the order. It's your signature. You bought the explosives, the same that were used on the Mancinis' construction site. You did the dirty work for the Biancos then, and now, because you never got out of that debt—when you basically sold your daughter to Bianco, and Al Mancini wouldn't have it."

"You think he cared about Sofia?" he all but spits out the words. "She was just a pawn in that game. You want to know who's pulling strings? Luca wasn't the only one cheating on his spouse. Ask Claudia about the time she slept with Frank Bianco. She found out one hell of a lot about him and his connections."

"Let's talk about those connections."

Dorman looks frustrated, but he hasn't interrupted us as much. Now, he speaks up.

"Arturo, they have a point. Agents, you better do this by the book. I want to know what you can offer my client first."

"Are you kidding me?" Arturo snaps at him. "Fuck that deal. They can't do anything for me, and you know why."

"They might." To Rachel and me, Dorman says, "I understand that you're looking to go much further than the Mancinis, or the old feud they had with my client and the Bianco family. If you're really interested in cleaning up once and for all, you better offer my client something good."

"How about you discuss this a bit more?" I suggest and get up.

Rachel shoots me a quizzical look, but she follows me outside the room.

"What is it? Things are going according to plan. This is where we want to be."

"Yes. I'm just not sure how much leeway we should give him."

"It was your idea, Johnson. What's the problem now?"

"Let's give him some time to think about it. If he's willing to provide names, and hard evidence, all right. I'd like to check something with Ms. Mancini first."

I don't like the look she gives me at all.

"What? He and Claudia have engaged in multiple ways to cut her out, and he did sign that purchase order. I want to make sure they don't try to wash their hands off this."

"Because there have been so many surprises with Kendall, or..." She lets her words trail off into an uncomfortable silence.

"I don't want any more surprises, period."

"Me neither. But Hampton can do it. I want you to stay here."

I don't like this at all though it's probably for the better. Kendall is likely still mad at me.

I knew better than to expect this situation to be resolved in a day. It's still making me nervous, the predictable time in limbo, not being able to talk to Kendall. I have a job to do. Those other times, *Catania*, the hotel suite, the getaway fortress, it all seems so unreal.

Yet, we were there. We said things that are hard to take back, and we meant them. At least I know I meant them. Can you actually love somebody and hardly ever be on the same page? It seems impossible.

There's a silver lining—the next few days will likely put an end to this case as we unravel all the connections between the players. Arturo and Claudia are back at home, and so am I.

Kendall isn't.

And realistically, I have no reason to feel sorry for her, or myself, but I do. After an hour at home, I leave my apartment again and walk to the metro station. From there, I take a train downtown and after a short walk, enter the place where we first met.

I first saw her in a crowded church where she swore to bring to justice the person who had killed her father and by proxy, her grieving mother as well.

The first time I ran into her was in this bar. It seems ages ago. I still can't believe how naïve I was, after a few undercover assignments under my belt, thinking I could come out of this without crossing lines. Not just to advance the case, but because I wanted to.

Because I wanted her.

I sit at the counter and order a Manhattan, pondering the recent developments. Arturo Rossi's involvement has cracked the case wide open. It's ironic. I don't look forward to telling Sofia.

And Dolan? He's been under the radar, hiding God knows where. I can't help thinking that he'll try to get back into business as soon as possible. If he can make a profit on hurting others, he will.

Fortunately, soon enough, we will arrest someone who might be able to help us.

Justifications. I have enough of them. I still feel guilty as I sip my drink, in freedom, while she is not.

But I can't have anyone else I love in danger. Whatever it takes to protect her—that is the plan.

Chapter
Twenty-Eight

I spend the better part of the next couple of days on details, a puzzle really, bit by bit until the picture emerges. It's stunning really, though nothing should surprise me anymore.

I have another meeting with Claudia and her lawyer. She, too, is in for some surprises.

"Wow. I had no idea how far this went. I swear. Frank and I...Well, we tried to avoid talking about business."

I can't imagine they were talking much at all, but that's irrelevant right now. The realistic prospect of ending up like her brother does wonders for her memory.

"Yes, we had these dinners, but I didn't know he was playing both sides. Son of a—" Resigned, she doesn't finish the sentence. "This goes far beyond Kendall and what happened with Uncle Alphonso, and Bruno."

"You're right about that," I say. "Look, he was never a friend of yours, or your family."

She sighs. "I wasn't in it to make friends. Kendall is wrong to let go of the high-end restaurant business. That was my incentive. I would have owned the biggest share."

"I'm afraid I don't know that much about your prospects, but I imagine it would make more sense to work with Kendall keeping the business together, no? She wants to slim it down, make it more efficient. And she would have had a place for you if you hadn't tried to kill her."

"I wanted her out, but not like that." Claudia shakes her head with vehemence. "Okay, so I realized that Arturo went far beyond what we had agreed on. I thought Kendall was making too many mistakes, but I never wanted her dead!"

It's fascinating how the stories are shifting. One central figure remains the same.

"You did the right thing by coming clean. You might have the chance to repair a lot of the damage and move on."

"How?" she asks, looking straight at me. "How can I hope to move on from this? I'm not sleeping with you, and even that wasn't enough to save Kendall from getting arrested."

"That has nothing to do with—" I remind myself that Rachel is watching. She knows that suspects will say anything, right? It's uncomfortable, to say the least. I made my decisions, and my peace, my feelings notwithstanding. "You will have the chance to talk things over with Kendall eventually. Meanwhile, the more you help us, the better for *you*."

"I got you, Agent," she says with a smirk. "Don't worry about it. It's not a secret to anyone, and so far, it doesn't seem to have hurt you. I'm serious, no need to worry. It looks like we have the same enemy. Enemies. Let's do this."

It's sort of amazing that families like the Mancinis and the Biancos thought they were running the city. There's an even deeper and uglier underbelly. Even if Al Mancini wanted to be one of the good guys, which is all relative in this context, they were all working within a corrupt system. The extent of it is staggering, but we are about to dismantle a big chunk of it.

"Yeah. Let's do this."

———ele———

With every passing minute, things look drearier for Rossi, and I'm not sorry. His son was in on the murder of Marina Fiori who gave information about Alphonso's death to Kendall. The Biancos set him up to take the fall by himself, but he's no innocent.

Arturo all but sold his daughter to them, and he never believed he did anything wrong. I don't care how long ago it was. I'm glad this is all finally catching up to them.

So far so good. Now we have to wait for the last moving part.

I'm nursing a coffee in the break room, wondering if Kendall will ever talk to me again. What our lessons were from all of it, and if there was ever a world in which we could be completely honest with each other, beyond the intimate part.

I did the right thing. For the public, for my career. It should feel different.

With a shrug I get up and pick up my coffee. At the door I turn around and get a bag of peanuts. It's going to be another long day. No communication with her.

Better that way.

———ele———

We are watching the moving parts carefully. Meanwhile, Winter & Dunne request another meeting as well.

"We want to know that you can assure the safety of our client," MacKenzie says sternly. It's not the first time she has said this.

"We have colleagues on site, ready to intervene."

"You think that's going to be enough, considering who we are dealing with?"

I've thought about this so many times, all eventualities, talked it through with Rachel, Ryan, and Hampton. They all agree. The sliver of a risk remains.

"These people need to be stopped," I tell her. "We have it under control."

Truth be told, it feels like the first time in the long time that things are under control, and it's a good feeling. Not every love story can have a happy ending, especially when it started on shaky ground to begin with. At least we'll do right by the people. That's all that matters. That's all that should matter.

When Hampton opens the door after a quick rap, he looks excited, and I know today is the day.

"Target's on the move," he says.

"That's good news. Ms. Winter, Ms. Dunne, thank you for your ongoing cooperation. We'll talk later."

MacKenzie Winter gives me a terse nod. I know that they, too, are eager to get this over with.

All the planning and risks taken in the last few days will finally amount to something.

Chapter
Twenty-Nine

W hen the guard tells me I have a visitor, hope
surges, treacherously, for a brief moment. Then
he gives me the name, and it all vanishes into nothing
again. MacKenzie and her partner have been in touch,
but I doubt they can do much. They have been vague
and evasive when it comes to my chances of getting out
of here soon—not a good sign.

To add insult to injury, the FBI, most notably Robyn,
doesn't seem to need me anymore. Perhaps they
reached an agreement with Claudia, or even Arturo
Rossi.

Silly me, I should have always known that it was a
possibility.

Robyn seemed so sincere when she questioned Judge
Collins' motives.

I have been depressed about many things in the past
few days. The fact that the woman who said she loved
me has all forgotten about me might be one of them. I
vary in my readiness to admit this, day to day, hour to
hour.

Speaking of Judge Collins though.

I'm curious. Why would he want to see me? To gloat? To pass on a message from Frank Bianco?

I don't care much for either alternative, but it's not like I have a lot of entertainment or even conversations in here. Solitary doesn't lend itself to that. For my own protection, of course. My parents made enemies over time, and so did I. It always seems to come down to the same people. Maybe Judge Collins can shed light on the situation.

The guard brings me to the room, which is not the common visiting area, and remains standing in the corner.

"Ms. Mancini. Good evening."

"Is it, Judge Collins? I have the feeling that if it wasn't for you, I might not be here."

"That's a very broad interpretation," he says with a jovial smile. "That deal you tried to make was always on shaky grounds."

"You came here just to tell me that?"

"Among other things, yes." He leans back into his chair comfortably, and waves to the guard who leaves the room. The sense of alarm I feel isn't paranoia. Collins has been a guest at dinners at my Uncle Lorenzo's house, and at the Biancos' as well. Sure, people like him navigate the territory, looking for a way in, the way Blake, Robyn's father did.

It doesn't mean that he's dirty to the core, but I've been burned too often.

"I assume you had the cameras cut as well. We can make this short. You want to be governor, I don't see how I could stop you, not that I was trying."

"Really, Kendall?" He leans close, the smile gone from his face. "That's not what I hear."

"What are you hearing? Humor me. I've spent the last few days in solitary confinement. You're aware I'm quite a bit out of the loop."

Collins laughs. It sounds bitter.

"Right. First Bruno and Frank Bianco, then your own cousins, finally Dolan and the Rossis. But you have nothing to do with all that."

"I'm not sure what you expect me to say. They all made bad decisions, and they came back to bite them."

"Is that so? Some people think you made the worst decisions of all." After a tense pause, he adds. "This is the end of the line, Kendall. You won't continue to mess with people's lives."

It all makes sense now—he's in over his head, and he blames me.

"So, the falling dominos have reached you. For what it's worth, I didn't know. I did what I had to in order to keep the business running."

"Maybe you're even telling the truth. It doesn't matter. You keep doing this, a lot more people will get hurt. It's my moral duty to put an end to it."

I would have liked to express my disgust at his hypocrisy but decide that can wait when he trains the gun on me. How the hell did he get a firearm in here?

"It's the guard's," Collins says proudly. "He will confirm that you attacked me, and he had to shoot you."

"With your prints on it? And this?" I raise my shackled hands, struggling to keep my voice calm. "You might have a lot of influence around here, but not that much. Someone will fold."

"Too bad it will be too late for you, Kendall."

He raises his arm.

It only takes a few seconds, though they are the longest of my life. Then the agents are in the room, yelling at him to drop the gun. I can see his wild expression, that of someone who's not used to losing. He is going to turn the weapon on himself, law enforcement or...me?

Before I can finish all those terrifying scenarios in my mind, they tackle him to the ground and arrest him.

"Thanks. That was a bit close though."

"You handled yourself well, Ms. Mancini," Rachel Carr says.

It's cold comfort. Robyn stands by the door. I catch her gaze, looking for...something. She turns to Ryan Farmer, speaking to her in hushed tones.

"Glad to be of help," I say, and I don't care if it sounds sarcastic. I was shot not long ago. I don't care to repeat the experience.

"What the hell are you doing?" Collins rages as Carr removes the shackles from my wrists. "That woman is dangerous! She tried to kill me!"

He pales when I open the jumpsuit, revealing the wire and the Kevlar vest.

"You will regret this!" He's beet red. "This will all come down on you."

"Oh, not again. This is getting old."

"I have to agree with Ms. Mancini. Get him out of here."

"This means nothing. It will be thrown out the moment—"

"Or maybe not." SAC Carr is content with herself and the outcome. "You really think this was a spontaneous effort? This is the tip of the iceberg. A large iceberg."

"Poetic," I comment, realizing I'm trembling, and I need to sit. "What happens next?"

━━ℓℓ━

I'm exhausted beyond measure when I finally return to my condo after these trying, boring days. It's not yet time to rest though, and I can't dwell on the fact that Robyn has barely spoken a word to me.

One phone call.

Then I order some pizza and settle in for the night to update my chief officers. I'll have to have more conversations with Winter & Dunne, too, sign more papers, but that can wait until tomorrow.

To my surprise, Claudia calls me. I consider not answering, but then decide I need a break, any break from the paperwork.

"I'm surprised," I say.

"Don't be. We both know I owe you an apology."

"That goes without saying. I'm surprised you want to. You seemed very adamant about doing business with Arturo."

"He's an asshole," she says dismissively. "Of course I knew that before, but he took it to new heights. I'm sorry, Kendall. I didn't mean for anyone to get hurt."

"It's a little late for that, but I hear you. Things got out of control."

"True." Her tone is wistful now. "I hope you can forgive me someday. I might be looking at some house arrest, but eventually, I'd love to help any way I can."

Robyn might be right to think some of us got off too easily—but that's the way it works. The Biancos, the Rossis, and now Judge Collins. They are working their way to the top, and whatever we liked to believe, Claudia or I weren't anywhere near. It appears we were useful though.

"We can talk about that, but honestly, I need a good night's sleep in my own bed."

"Of course. You could come to dinner next week?"

"Sure."

If that sounds vague, I can't help it. I'm going to have to face Luca as planned. I'm going to face a lot of uncomfortable truths, one at a time. Not tonight though.

Instead of turning in, I take another long hot shower and dress for a night out. I know just the place to go.

ℓℓℓ

"Hey, Kendall, how's it going?" the bartender greets me as if my family hasn't been in the headlines constantly for months.

"Not too bad," I say as I sit on the barstool. I got a few admiring looks coming in. That felt good, though I'm not looking for affirmation. Just a couple of drinks and a sentimental trip down memory lane. "You?"

"Same old," she responds with a shrug. "The usual? You're expecting anyone?"

"Yes and no. Hate to disappoint you."

She doesn't comment but goes to fix my drink. She's quick and efficient, and luckily for me, has to tend to another customer right after, a woman that's a bit chattier. Good. I need some time to reflect. It would make a lot more sense to do that after sleep, but here I am.

Will this finally be the end of it? As far as acute danger goes, probably. The FBI will unravel the spider web Judge Collins has woven with the Biancos, the cover-up, the connections, all of it.

I can finally go back to some sort of normalcy.

Whatever that will look like.

I sense her presence before she leans in, wrapping her arms around me from behind and resting her head against my back.

She must be tired, too, of keeping secrets from everyone, for the greater good. But it's not like either one of us has a choice.

"I wasn't sure you'd come," I say. She lets go, reluctantly, as it seems, and I turn to her, all but stumble from the stool and into her embrace.

"I'm not going to apologize."

"I didn't think you would. I understand very well what's on the line for you."

"Do you?"

"I'm a bit insulted that you're still questioning it."

With a sigh, Robyn reaches for my glass and takes a sip.

"I could get you your own."

"That would be appreciated."

I signal the bartender, pointing to the glass. She gives me the thumbs up and starts to prepare another one.

"I came here to tell you that you are now free. We both are. You can go back to taking care of business." Given her serious tone and expression I can't help but worry there's more. "I also came here to tell you we shouldn't meet again, not in this way."

It's not that much of a surprise, but I'm dismayed she got as far as saying it out loud.

"How is that working out for you?"

Robyn thanks the bartender and takes the first sip. And another.

"As you can see, not at all. I can't be with someone who tells me lies, even if they think it's to protect me. Or someone who will disappear without a warning."

"I wouldn't do that to you."

She raises an eyebrow, and I clarify. "The latter anyway. I can't pretend I always told you the truth, at least not right away. That goes both ways, doesn't it? I know you'll tell me your omissions are more justified because of your job, but I couldn't be so sure about where we stood either."

"Still not apologizing, and you're right. I couldn't always tell you everything, because it was too dangerous. We had to make Collins believe that you had nothing left to lose, and that you would use everything you had against him."

"I'd say that went well." I can't help the hint of sarcasm. She seems genuinely sorry. I am too, for not seeing through the entirety of the ruse.

"When I set up the sting with Carr, I had to stay at a distance. I had to make him trust me, so he would let his guard down. I couldn't risk anyone finding out..."

She lets her words trail off, and I finish them for her.

"That you care about me?"

Robyn doesn't deny it.

"I owed you an explanation. I'm not sorry for doing my job and bringing this to an end."

"So, you expect me to take you home simply because you're irresistible?"

She gives me a long look over the rim of her glass.

"Are you saying there's a chance?"

I shake my head, laughing. "Best laid plans and all. My security system is updated, and besides, the bad guys are behind bars. Let's go home? The drinks aren't as pricey anyway."

"Come on, Kendall! I heard that!" the bartender comments.

Of course that was a joke. Everything I have at home is a bit more pricey than what they serve here. My offer, though, was not. Robyn is right. We are apparently unable to keep our distance. Why fight it?

All of a sudden, I'm not tired any longer.

Chapter Thirty

I didn't mean to return to the bar or speak to Kendall when I saw her sitting at the counter. Who am I kidding? I've been missing her so much. I know I hurt her, but I had no choice. All of my points are valid though. There have to be some ground rules, I think as she traces a finger down my naked back, making me shiver with pleasures received and anticipated. We'll have to sleep at some point, but it's not now.

"I am sorry," I whisper. Here in the dark, in the privacy of these safe surroundings, we can finally tell the whole truth.

"I know." She kisses me softly, then with renewed passion, and pulls me close. I'll have many more opportunities to make it up to her, to apologize for letting her think I'd abandoned her, and every one of them is pure sensual delight.

When we fall asleep, it's not with utmost clarity, but at least knowing that no one will try to invade the condo tonight.

I am woken by my cell phone, late enough for the sun to be high in the sky already. I don't care for disengaging myself from Kendall's embrace, but it keeps ringing.

"What is so important right now? You know I'll be coming in later today," I say to Hampton.

"We got a tip on Dolan," he says. "When we got to the address, he was there..." That little pause can't mean anything good. "Dead."

"That's...regrettable, but why are you calling me? He's a high-profile drug dealer, of course he made some enemies. Can I still come in later, or do you absolutely need me now?"

It's not that I'm not curious.

"Come in as planned. I just wanted you to know."

I sit up and put my feet on the floor, cell phone still in hand.

"Bad news?" Kendall asks softly. I shrug.

"It's Dolan. Looks like somebody murdered him. The timing is strange. I guess I should go."

"I was hoping we could have breakfast together."

"I'm sorry. Another time. I swear." I turn back to her and kiss her. Pulling back after a few sweet, sexy moments, I ask, "You didn't have anything to do with that, right?"

"Why would you think that? They just let me out of prison. I don't have magic powers."

"You didn't answer my question."

"And you're asking too many." She yawns. "I'm sorry, but I really need some coffee now. You're sure you can't stay?"

"I'm sure. Sorry. I'll come by later if that's all right with you?"

Her expression is amused. "That's more than all right. I'll see you then."

ﾟﾟﾟﾟﾟﾟ

"You're here, good," Rachel greets me. "I guess you heard about Dolan?"

"Yes, Hampton told me."

"Okay. We'll assist the local PD on this and, of course, keep the big picture in mind."

"Of course," I echo, as I suppress a sigh of relief. I was almost worried she'd ask me about Kendall. Kendall who has promised me time and again that it would take only one phone call, and she knew I was tempted...

But it's so much better to give in to another kind of temptation. It would be easy to get lost in the memory of last night...but I won't, not with my boss standing right in front of me.

"Um, is there anything else?"

"Hampton will bring you up to date on the Dolan case, but I'd like you to come with me and meet someone."

"Sure. What's the occasion?"

"Given what's happened in the past few weeks, I've decided that we could use another expert consultant. Someone who's knowledgeable about what's going on in the rival crime families, what's left of them."

"Sound good to me. Who is it?"

Rachel opens the door to an office and steps aside to let me in. I walk inside, doing a double-take when I realize who she's talking about.

"Since you already know each other, we can get to work right away."

"Agent Johnson. I look forward to working with you—again."

Kendall gets to her feet and meets me halfway to shake my hand, holding on to it a bit longer than necessary.

Looks like we're in it for the long haul.

"So do I," I say.

About the Author

Barbara Winkes writes suspense and romance with lesbian characters at the center. She has always loved stories in which women persevere and lift each other up. Expect high drama and happy endings. Women loving women always take the lead.

Acknowledgements

Dominique, for always being along for the journey from a vague idea to the actual book.

May Dawney for another gorgeous cover.

My fellow authors for continuing to answer my never-ending questions, and for their amazing stories.

To all the readers who enjoyed the beginning of Kendall & Robyn's story, and came back for more.

Thank you so much! This adventure couldn't happen without you.

Printed in Great Britain
by Amazon

55909915R00121